the village on horseback

Also by Jesse Ball

Fiction
The Curfew
Samedi the Deafness
The Way Through Doors

Verse & Prose
March Book
Vera & Linus

Drawings
Og svo kom nóttin

the village on horseback

PROSE AND VERSE, 2003–2008

JESSE BALL

milkweed
editions

The characters and events in this book are fictitious. Any similarity to real persons, living or dead, is coincidental and not intended by the author.

© 2011, Text by Jesse Ball
All rights reserved. Except for brief quotations in critical articles or reviews, no part of this book may be reproduced in any manner without prior written permission from the publisher: Milkweed Editions, 1011 Washington Avenue South, Suite 300, Minneapolis, Minnesota 55415.
(800) 520-6455
www.milkweed.org

Published 2011 by Milkweed Editions
Printed in Canada
Cover design by Jeenee Lee Design
Cover photo, "Bergers à La Mouleyre, Commensaq" by Felix Arnaudin. Used with permission from Musée d'Aquitaine © Mairie de Bordeaux
Interior design by Connie Kuhnz
The text of this book is set in Cochin.
11 12 13 14 15   5 4 3 2 1
First Edition

Please turn to the back of this book for a list of the sustaining funders of Milkweed Editions.

Library of Congress Cataloging-in-Publication Data

Ball, Jesse, 1978–
     The village on horseback / Jesse Ball. — 1st ed.
          p.   cm.
     Includes bibliographical references and index.
     ISBN 978-1-57131-442-0 (alk. paper)
     I. Title.
     PS3602.A596V55 2011
     811'.6—dc22

                                        2011013691

This book is printed on acid-free paper.

For Catherine Ball

THE VILLAGE ON HORSEBACK

Postmen like doctors go from house to house.

—P. Larkin

Grateful Acknowledgement is given to the editors of the following journals where these poems previously appeared:

"A Set Piece," *The Boston Review.*

"Morceau" and "And if They Should Tell You," *Conduit.*

"Speech by a Window," "Speech in a Chamber," "Speech Confided," "Speech in a Meadow," "Auturgy," *The Paris Review.*

"A Turn," "A Calico Ascription," "Report From Our Lands," "That Season," *Oberon.*

"Balloon Diary, Week of the Pastoral Revolt" "Asking Advice of the Scissors," "The Distressing Effect of Rumors," *Denver Quarterly.*

"Here is some information about turtles," *Hobart.*

"A Project," *Conduit.*

"Parables & Lies," *The Cupboard Pamphlet.*

"The Early Deaths of Lubeck, Brennan, Harp & Carr" *The Paris Review.*

"Pieter Emily," *Guernica.*

INTRODUCTION

The works included in this volume were written between 2003 and 2008. During that time I lived (in 2003–2004) in a series of Manhattan and Brooklyn apartments, (in 2004–2006) in various parts of France, (in 2006–2007) in Iceland, and lastly, (in 2007–2008) in Chicago. Matching the places up to the works is most likely a ridiculous proposition, but I encourage those who choose to do it.

It has always been my ambition to produce an omnibus, a small, tidy book of depths that would fit in a pocket, yet occupy a traveler for several train rides. When I saw that these various books of mine could come together into such an omnibus, I was delighted, and went forward with the idea immediately. What you have before you is the result of that thought.

Jesse Ball, 6 April 2011

the village on horseback

parables and lies

2003

They were given the choice of becoming kings or kings' messengers. As is the way with children, they all wanted to be messengers. That is why there are only messengers, racing through the world and, since there are no kings, calling out to each other the messages that have now become meaningless.

F. Kafka   2 Dec. 1917

The Coming Upon A Play

If you were to go walking on a certain day, intent on winning the heart of a certain girl, you might invite her to walk with you along the river road. She might consent, and climbing out her tiny window, she would leap down into your arms, and together you would go. But never would you imagine that there by the river, a cast of actors is awaiting the rise of an enormous curtain which no one can see, and that they are waiting for none other than the two last actors, who straggle, many hours away, along some country road. By chance, they resemble you and your love exactly. By chance, you arrive just as the curtain rises.

The Palace

A palace so large that the kingdom itself is but a small part of it. Servants sent to some far corridor are given burials, for we know well that they will not return. Communication is a matter of whispers, which travel like cursed fact. And our hearts are maintained through windows, where courtesans' soft skin and long lashes are arguments that uphold this life. Everyone has their orders, which must be carried out. These are kept in tiny cylinders hung like pendants from our servile necks. Since we cannot read, we must ask others to read these instructions for us. And often these interpretations change. All in all it is a good way to be, or so I have heard, as beyond the walls of this enthronement there are great doubts like standing trees, and each outlives a man, and each is named for some task we will never be allowed.

A Bird's Judgment

You have been betrayed. Yes, it's true. It's early September in the city where you live and someone has spoken to the authorities. Even now, the chief of police is sitting behind an enormous mahogany desk in the vast ministry, waiting for you to be brought in. All across the city, squads of officers are preparing themselves. Likenesses of your face are being handed out.

It's true you meant no harm. Also true: there's no way anyone could know. And yet the real truth remains: someone has given you up. Soon there will be boot-steps on the stairs, a loud knocking at the door. Soon you will be spoken to repeatedly in a loud voice, tied and carried under a policeman's arm like a parcel to a waiting car.

If only you could make it into the next apartment and beg your life of the widow who lives there, she would hide you, and then how happily and well you would live. But even to stir from your chair is impossible. For the book of your acquaintance has closed on this hundred-hundredth day, and limp clouds are straggling like children across the windowpane. There is no hope. You have been betrayed and the wild exodus of fate from the fated is never-begun and always-finished. The sounds from the street are maddeningly normal. Also, it's hotter than you like, and you are wearing far too many clothes. As if a bird told a bird a bird's judgment, the day itself has announced its coming in yellow colors and vague shapes just beyond the edge of sight.

A Visitor

A green sea, huge and fugitive, sits at anchor beneath the roof of your small home. Word of this is general in the village, and neighbors pass by again and again hoping for a glimpse. But your bemusement is like a well-worn knife and you caress it slowly, back turned, as a tiny smile plays against the broom closet, pretending it is a broom, though in truth you know, it is no such weighty thing.

Banditry

In among the foregone on the narrow road that circles and recircles the city of your tongue, the highwayman has gone walking with his next victim. He is handsome and dashing; she is young and petulant. They stop beneath a tree and her long hair falls to the ground. She says, "I am in love with a man, but I fear he is a bandit." To this the man says nothing, but stands, quietly stroking her hair. A cold breeze rises and he holds her close. Soon in the distance he will see evening riding and know that it is time.

A Lark

By the harbor, a great work has begun. We of this town already think of ourselves differently. Travelers have started to arrive. They say they left their homeland years ago at the news, and have been on the roads for generations. When it is finished this statue will be a portrait-signature upon an uncertain earth, a letter we few shall leave for the crowded centuries that wait inside the hills. And to think, I know the headman, who used to be the town's mason. I spoke to him, saw him pass in the street just days ago. He was head-to-toe in flat working gray, and could be missed but for the fiendish cast of his eyes. And who but a mad man could make such a statue? A statue of the town in which we live, exact and equal to an inch, yet formed from the hardest stone and rising up out of the water. Already it looms above the town on great marble stilts. I saw myself walking there, or standing as it were, as I once walked, beside a pond with lilies. He saw me, he must have seen me walking there, where I often walked, by that pond where my daughter was drowned. And yes, in the waters of the marble pond, I see he has etched some impression of a face looking up from the depths. He has peopled the houses with scenes from our lives. He has stretched the avenues, and laid them with old parades and angry, roused evenings. In the center square, on which work has just begun, a man is being lynched. But best of all, at the harbor mouth of the statue town, which will come last, he tells me will be built a marble sea in which we all shall be buried, one by one, as years and hours take our hands.

The Bank of Perth

It is rumored to exist in every city, in every human settlement. One has heard, or one knows of someone who has heard, in the crowded street, in the drawing-rooms of wealth, in the merchants' salons and the workmen's meeting houses, the timbre of an agent of the Bank, facilitating advance, supplying the necessary collateral, acceding to wishes, and accounting, irrefutably, for all the gaps in our human exchanges. Where do such agents come from? How may they be known? They seem never to be seen, but would be recognized at once. Often they can be made out, barely, across a room, in closeted discussion with some luminary. One presses closer, and the bank agent is gone. Furthermore, no one saw him go.

Not to the natural world, nor to celestial orders are such intentions bound. The Bank of Perth cannot be countermanded, is greater than the sum of all countries, for though every country has fallen and will fall, the Bank cannot fall, nor fail. Its location need not be secret, and yet it cannot be known. All currency is dispensed in its favor, and greed is the tool of its want.

Several times in our long history, a mystic or true philosopher has unearthed the deepest secrets of the Bank of Perth. But even to do this is to go beyond use, for those who have seen such sights may never speak of them, may never tell of them, may never treat of them. Save, of course, in parable.

The Suitors

A man was out taking the summer air when along the lane he saw a crowd approaching. Perhaps not a crowd. They were arrayed in a line, and each suitor was grander in dress and manner than the one who came before. The line stretched endlessly, over hill and dale. On the farthest hilltop, the man could see the crowns of kings and the scepters of emperors glinting in the sunlight. Where are they going? he inquired of the first, but his question went unanswered. Where are you going?

he asked again. The man did not join the line, but went humbly beneath his roof and began to prepare for himself the smallest of meals, which he would eat without haste by the window, which he would eat with a tiny wooden spoon, making no noise that one might hear, were one to pass that way.

The Seamstress of Bao Suk

There was once in Bao Suk, at the end of a certain unmentionable dynasty, a seamstress living and working in a shop near the gates of the city. Her daughters were lovely and useless, but would serve to wear the clothing that she made, that it might be seen and sold to any who passed by. Her fame had grown over the course of a difficult life, difficult not by any curse of fortune, for indeed, her star had always risen, but difficult because her wishes were not the wishes of her fellow men and women, her ambitions were couched in an obscure turn of thought. As a child she had wandered far and wide with her old father through the mountain range which girdled that ancient piece of land. Of it no good can be said, and even in our modern times, the most scientific of men avoid the treacheries and infidelities of those nameless peaks. In her eighth year, on one such sojourn, she left her father sleeping, and went alone into places even he, faultless and intrepid man that he was, would not go. There she was told the things that she must in the sun, the man had been planning the house, and he had come to the decision that his house should have but one door, as was the custom in those parts. Now the laborer's wife was a lovely woman, and had been the prize of the district until she had taken his hand and let him lead her beneath the marriage arch. This was a strange thing, accounted strange by all concerned, for the laborer's wife could have had any man, rich or poor, but of them all, she had chosen him. And it was not for his looks, nor for his wits, nor for his temper, as the laborer would in none of these ways impress. No, she had married him because of a certain child that had grown in the dark, deep inside her, and which, when she was aware of it, had told her by kicking and scraping that if she would be safe and whole and living, she should at once be married. And so she had done; the child arrived, and 3 long years had passed, living within the house of the laborer's father, day and night, forever beneath the watchful eye of the laborer's mother, who wondered day and night, why had she, the local beauty, married her plain son. And when the time came for their own house to be built, she had told her husband that they must have two doors, one to the east and one to the west, that the sun might be let in in the morning, and let out at nightfall. One door or two, the laborer asked himself, as he walked up and down in the fields. One door or two, he asked himself again, as he trudged home through a patchwork of hills. For his mother had told him, day in day out, you must watch a pretty wife. You must watch her with both of your god-given eyes, and with the others too, that are little spoken of. For she will squirm in your arms, and tell you that she is yours, but my son, beauty cannot be kept. It is restless, and will speak to every passing eye, will allow the lissome stares of every passing man.

One door or two. One door or two. It was to be but a one-room house. And as she says, day and night, the sun must be allowed to pass. Not just through all the broad and empty places, but through this town of man, and through that town of man, through anger and misfortune, through pettiness and filth. And every sun will be a deeper, a crueler sun. And every sun will know far better the shape, the broad dull shape, of the wound it makes on your face and arms, the wound it presses, deep through the windows of your eyes, where such things will be remembered, but can never be made good.

Trickery

He had two little ones in his care. There there, he would say, and hold them one at a time, pressed up against his chest or leg. How they loved such times! With trumpeting cries they would race away and back. Were they children? Were they capable of such a brutal thing as

A Letter

Everyone has moved away or died, but you are still quite young. You bathe each day in the salt sea, and ring your lonely shack with twined cornflowers. You are, it is said, expecting a visitor. If the others don't speak of it, it is because there are no others. There's no one but you, and you are too young to know how completely you have been beaten.

Before the Emperor

There were once two clowns who traveled the land. They would never be seen in the same city, nor would they speak of each other. However their hatred was a known thing, and everyone longed to see what would happen if they were brought together in one place. Many stories circulated about their hate, regarding how it was begun, and why. Some said they were brothers, others that they were father and son. Both were the favorites of equally prominent noblemen, and so one might not be humbled before the other without calling higher powers into contention.

However, it became the will of the people that the two clowns be brought together unawares, on the great stage of the Capital. It was the will of the Emperor of course, and had little to do with the people. Yet the Emperor was in the habit of calling his will the people's, and so I have told it thus.

In any case, the clowns were assembled, one in each wing, each thinking his was the only act. The curtains were pulled, the clowns emerged, to stand face to face, as the Emperor watched from his box, surrounded by his retinue, as the massed nobles pressed up against the fur-trimmed stage, as the merchants peered through opera glasses from the far corners of the theater. . . .

Well they were not clowns. It is not known who they were. They did not know each other. They did not know anyone. And when they met on the stage, they did nothing but stand with unpainted faces staring at the thousand jeering heads that slandered the air. But of course, no one spoke. The theatre was entirely silent.

The first clown took a sharp knife from the little bag he had been given. From a seated position, he carefully cut his feet off at the ankles, cradling first the left foot, then the right. He took the severed feet, and gently placed them in his bag. His face was calm. The stumps of his red legs wept a steady stream, passing the time, and he was soon asleep.

The second clown drew a whistle from the folds of his coat, and blew three long notes. An enormous bird jumped from the crowd and snatched the clown's head from off his shoulders before galloping like a horse three times around the stage. At this point, it was speared by a daring young man who attended the Emperor. The headless clown had fallen from beheading into a kneeling position, hands folded before him.

The crowd was hushed. What did the Emperor think of all this? He had the clowns skinned and had the skins made into costumes which he would wear in alternation to the many costume balls it was his habit to give in the winter season. Of course, from the one skin-suit his head stuck out, and from the other his feet. Therefore the Emperor was always recognizable, which is proper and correct, and prevents terrible mistakes from being made on the part of the foolish or the brave.

An Argument I Chanced To See

It was never and it was nevertheless along a poor and thoughtless line of thought that we had come. There were no longer shopkeepers. There were no longer shops. What it did mean to us? We were forced to make all our own things. Thus we became shabby and kind, and famous in a silly, stupid way. Seven ideas were listed in a book that came to light part way through the emergency. But the eldest of us, Gustav, would have none of it, and took the book away to his room where no one else dared go. What am I going on about? What question was I asked? Ah yes, you, you with the long gloves, come forward. Speak, man! Ask a question of this survivor of the foreign, who stands before you in his smallclothes. Armed struggles are never difficult. It is peace that lays countries low. And the lowest of them, this sinking star

of my failed fame, it drips with ordure. IF I MUST walk
to the next town on foot, I will, but please . . . I repeat,
tonight I will tell you STORIES, and in exchange you'll
let me sleep inside your house.

A System of Letter-Writing

All the letters were dated, either with the date the letter
was sent, or with the date it was received. They went
into a series of cabinets built expressly for that pur-
pose and set against a low wall behind which at certain
hours of the day, one might see the sun setting. The
letters were written in a bent scrawl which somehow
managed to be perfectly legible. From a distance it al-
most looked like Arabic or Sinhalese. Up close, it was
all too clear. One couldn't begin reading the letters,
because if one did, hours would pass and one would
have accomplished none of the tasks that had been set.
Oh, it was all too easy to spend the day rummaging
and filing, all night reading and rejoicing. For in these
letters, these peculiar letters of a most unpublic, un-
admired man, were hidden tortuous machinations and
intricate apparatuses of invention. Of course, the dif-
ficulty lay not in setting the letters in order, for they
were already in order, but in putting them out of order.
For the man had employed us specifically for that pur-
pose. He wanted no letters of similar subject to remain

beside one another. He wanted no date congruent, no place-name beside itself. For physicians had told him he would die on the eighth day of the third month of his sixtieth year and towards that day he was preparing a scheme of complication that his legacy might be a lure to fortune seekers and puzzle solvers. He was not known as an author, yet in his letters were hidden many novels of curious scholarship. He was not known as a scientist, yet in his letters he had concealed equations and documented experiments which would revolutionize many sectors of our uniformed existence. Not a banker, nor an economist, he nonetheless knew the hermetics of currency. Not a statesman nor a saint, he nonetheless made speeches (gone unheard) that gave to the human soul the dignity it lacks. He was not a baker or an engineer, yet he devised ovens which would bake as no oven ever had, and breads that might be baked within such an oven, breads the likes of which you have never tasted.

And perhaps you never will, for my friends and I, we are a wily bunch, and we have had years with which to tortuate our master's genius. And all the years we have been spoiling and hiding, concocting and puzzling. In his maze of letters there will seem little to be found, though truly, as I have said, there is little in fact that might not be found in this seething bath, this system of letters that will be alluded to in the final sentence of the final article of an interminable and indiscriminate will.

Parable of the Lamp

A man may have been in the business of burying the dead, and he may have buried them, day in, day out, for decades, such decades beginning sometimes in the gray of dusk, and ending, too often, in the early murmur of dawn's foundering cascade. He may have kept his shovel close by the bed, or propped safe against a near wall, cleaned it gently at nightfall with a wet rag, oiled it in off moments, laid by. He may have spoken in this life more often to an object than to a person, more often with question than with conviction. He may have stood for hours on a rain-swept slope, admiring neat rows of stone markers, absent of mourners. And he may have begun a long tale, a new part of which he would invent each night as he sat alone at table.

The facts are uncertain. We have only the book with which to decipher the life, however fictional. He certainly lived, and certainly, quite certainly, he died. That lamp which stands between ourselves and a brighter lamp often seems less like a lamp and more like a hooded man. Thus we inquire of him, from where have you come? Thus we throw wide our doors and set out all that is left in the pantry. Do so with an eking touch, and sparingly, for in the book of names, all names are not entered. Our lies are precautions. Our sentinels are doubts that dredge a living sea.

A Badger told a Rat

And how fine it would be, if, at the end of a life, one could seek congratulation from all those one knew in the circumstances of childhood, as it were, within those very circumstances, when such congratulations, forming, as they would, the basis for a life, would have been worthwhile.

The Infant Elsbet

Oh, too often we hear tell of the infant Elsbet, who is found here or there in the night or morning. She is carried, wrapped in a shawl, back to the cottage where she lives, and set again within her gilded cradle. Yet always she escapes, in light and dark, to wander the hills on her hands and knees, tiny mouth panting, tiny eyes asquint. She is accounted good luck by the fishermen, who find her often on the path to the daybreak wharf. Others think less of her, and treat her more roughly, speak to her with a colder tongue. Why does she never grow? Why do her garments never stain? Who keeps the cottage where she lives, who feeds her? The town sits in the shadow of a distant mountain to which no one has ever gone. On gray porches, stern wives negotiate the wool of half-formed garments, wielding impossibly sharp needles. Along the street, someone is calling, "Elsbet is gone again. Elsbet is gone." Be sure she will be found.

A Statuette

He took my statuette. I saw him. He led himself a pretty
path right up the middle of the street, and stopping at
my door, he knocked. Seeing no one was home (for
I was hiding beneath my bed), he entered and passed
through all the various rooms, coming finally into my
own, where upon a small night table the statuette was
placed. Oh statuette of a tearful god! How long I had
kept you close beside me while I slept. But he put you
under his coat, with one quick movement of a slim-
fingered hand, and off he went.

I thought for a moment, as he stood above me, of com-
ing out from beneath the bed and making my presence
known. But it seemed the wrong thing to do. Questions
would be raised. What, for instance, was I doing beneath
my bed on that miserable and immemorial day?

The Hospital

Inside the hospital there were several villages. I lived
in the first, in a small cottage with my sister. We were
not allowed to go to the other villages, nor were they
allowed to come to us. But news was always circulat-
ing regarding the escape of a villager from one place or
another.

How long had we lived in the village? This was a
question I posed constantly to my sister. We would sit,

glazed eyes mimicking glazed eyes, and mouth answers which we dared not speak. When we had first arrived, my sister insisted on saying we had lived there always. Now that we had lived there always, she insisted on saying that we had just arrived. Her skinny arms hung off the sides of her stiff wooden chair, which she kept trying to rock as if it was a rocker. The artist who had drawn her face must have watered down his ink fearing he would run out, for her features were indistinct — almost absent. She would only wear the one color, a pale yellow, and she thought herself a great beauty, though she had never told anyone this. She was always tempting me, slipping into my bed halfway through the night, or groveling at my feet.

The rest of the villagers hated us. They felt we were newcomers and should be hurt at every opportunity. But we had been there longer than anyone, and refused to allow their tawdry claims. After I put a fellow through a plate-glass window, they left me alone. But my sister was too delicate. I'd find her, huddled somewhere, bruised and crying, her yellow clothes torn. Once, I saw her running naked along the riverbank, chased by four old women. Together we drowned them, and used their clothing for scarecrows in our yard.

Always of an evening, my sister would be tapping at the glass with her fingertips, as I sat composing elaborate logical proofs that might one day prove there were no other villages but ours. I suppose she meant the same by her tapping as I did by my proving. Once, she turned to me, face filthy from contact with our matted floor, and said, "Of all the villages, ours is the most easily understood. Each successive village is less believable. Each is worse. Even so much as a thought arrived at bravely can mean your expulsion from one place, your inclusion in another."

"But what," I asked her, "did we think of, to bring us here?"

"Brother of mine, we looked in every cabinet and under every tree for the way back to an earlier village. But with each passage we fall faster."

With that she removed her dress and began to rub herself against the curtain. Then I realized, the tapping was continuing, but she was not tapping. Looking up, first at this window, then at that, I saw that behind every pane of glass there was an uglier and more spiteful face, beneath which gripped and ungripped, tapped and tapped and tapped again, the many fingers of a great and angry crowd.

Mention

And to think, of all the great and wonderful things that could have happened . . . that your name should have been mentioned, and by whom and to whom! Now you are sorry for all the terrible things you did when the world seemed an unkind place. Now you recoil from your darker period, that time which preceded this glorious day. No more shall you sit alone in windswept cafes as rain broods over dim cities. No more shall you stand for hours outside your own terrible door, outside the doors of others. No, no . . . you have been mentioned, spoken well of before company, and it is plain to all — your life has acquired the glorious sheen of reputation before which all else must inevitably fall.

A Scene

Day draws to a close. One man passes another in the street, and as they pass, each looks the other in the face, as if to say, "You may indeed be the center of all this, but sir, it is just as likely I should be." Nearby, a painfully soft little bird has alighted on a branch, watching the comings and goings with great interest. And you and I, we arrive later to that moment, and thus cannot be noticed, nor gainsaid, as we make our way along the thin streets of that decades-lost foundry town. Equally, we can be certain both men were quite wrong.

An Emerald

It came to be known that one of the miners in that filthy godforsaken camp had found an emerald as big as a

man's fist. The jealousy of the other miners. The plea-
sure of the miner's wife. The worry of the miner himself
over the possible theft of his newfound prize.

And how he woke the next day and the day after
from dreams in which it had not been he who found the
gem, but another. And how nothing could be done to
.comfort him but that the emerald should be brought out
from its hiding place, and that he should be let to touch
it and hold it and wake fully from his dream with all the
glory of this true plane upon his dirty lap.

Claus Valta

During the golden age of punishment, peasants often dreamed secretly of a brutal public death that might earn some measure of fame. The greatest of the executioners, Claus Arken Valta, was much in demand, and would tour the country with a coach and horses, sleeping each night in a golden pavilion. He wore a moustache, though it was not the style, and always bathed his hands in a bowl of milk that would be set beside his axe, or laid nearby the gibbet. He had a fine voice and could carry many a pleasant tune. Often he would sing as he went about hitching up horses for the drawing and quartering of a felon or wastrel. He took pity on everyone, and would cry if he saw a bird with a broken wing, or a three-legged dog stumbling through the crowd. At such times he was inconsolable, and would refuse to go on with the execution. Afterwards, always, he repented and would slaughter as many as nine or ten deserving souls in as many minutes. His penchant for public speaking was exceeded only by his memory for faces. "Why, haven't I seen you before?" he would remark, as he tightened a noose around some unfortunate's neck. Without waiting for an answer, he'd loose the trap and watch the bagheaded wretch drop to a wrenching death. He rarely let the dying have their last words before the crowd, instead gagging them, and inventing speeches which they might have said, the which he would recite to the crowd from memory. In this he was no different from other great men. What they imagine is always more palpable, more true, than anything we might wish or wish to say.

Of the Secret City

AND if on the banks of that river to which you once did go, there arose a fair city, of which you alone could know—how sad that this knowledge has eluded you, how sad that you have lived so long from home, spendthrift of your life until even *this* has abandoned you, even this hidden city, never seen, has faded out of possibility into such a realm as the one in which we now speak.

Parable of Life's Wake

—A woman who has just smothered the man with whom she slept. The disarray of her clothing. Her steps, back and forth in that tiny room. Light is beginning by the window, intending to cross slowly as it always has done. If the woman were to scream, and someone, anyone, were to come to her assistance, how much could she hope for from such a person? Might they help her to hide her crime? Might they take advantage of her in this, her weakness? If she should sigh and toss her pretty head, and pass through the town in crinoline, gold glittering on her thumbs and ankles, why, who could tell her different? Who could say, "You may not do this that you have done." For life is its own excuse, its wake the shed gray, the unbearable touch of the harshest wool.

Unnoticed Offenses

One man said: I refuse to be seen with such a person!

He spoke of you.

I wonder what you did, unknowingly, to make him hate you so. I wonder who else, unknowingly, you have made enemies of, on this and other days. And of them, who will wait in the wings of your moving theatre, trembling and grinning, anticipating a later scene or act?

To Knock at an Unknown Door

A wealthy man went walking one day, on the grounds of his great estate. He walked in familiar places, admiring first this view, then that. He ranged farther from the manse until, as the sky began to darken, he realized he was walking in a region of his lands where he had never been. Through a veil of trees, he saw a tiny cottage; in the window were lighted candles which seemed to welcome him.

Such a man, such an estate, such a cottage (near and yet impossibly removed from all else, come to only at dark and in confusion)—out of this what is possible? What is not?

The man approached the cottage and with the boldness of a landowner stamped his feet loudly upon the doorstep and knocked upon the door.

It was a moment before anything happened, but when things began, it seemed they happened all at once. The door flew open—behind it was a man, in face and manner identical to the landowner. With a sneer and a shout, he drove an iron poker straight through the wealthy man's chest, and with a second roar withdrew it, stepping forward to catch the body as it fell. Discarding the poker, he pulled the body back into the house, drawing shut the door in one clean motion. Not even a cry had escaped the landowner's mouth. Door shut, the cottage stood again in silence, its windows candlelit, the season pressing in on all sides. It is possible, the candles seemed to say, that a double may stay in hiding at your heel for decades, and that one day you may come upon him. A man may not resist his double.

Late in the evening, a landowner who had been out walking returned, and advanced up the tree-lined carriage drive before his elegant house. He paused repeatedly, as if to admire each thing, each object of his vision as though all were new to him. At the door he was greeted by a servant, who took his coat and led him to table, where his wife and children awaited him. Servants saw to his every need.

Mutterings

Do not come near when flood waters are rising. It was in foolishness that our hearts were overthrown, and it will be in haste that our lives end. A set of toys, laid out on some inarticulate floor, will be like causes in a causeless time. Ask why, as if in doubt. Doubt is a glorious luxury, and one upon which we base all our hopes. Upon a silver field, motley hunters have speared a boar. The composition shakes and trembles, as wind moves from object to comparison.

The Book

In the book she wrote down things that were surely true and things that were surely false. Nothing was subject to interpretation—this was the necessary wrong, with great freedom the result. She wrote, *a man has hurriedly leapt from coveted position, and found surfeit of disaster,* then stopped, looking out an open window to where two boys were piling rocks. *Upon those of our own breath, we heap the hardest, heaviest stone.* A knock came then, with a letter pushed beneath the door. She took it to the bed, and drawing her knees up to her chest, read the letter spread out before her on the bed.

My dear, my darling,

I have been told by those who now manage my affairs, that I may never see you again. would that it were not so, and yet it seems maybe that we may each accomplish what we need to best in the other's absence.

I remain, yours,

X

She rocked back and forth with drawn features, and sobbed once. Yet soon she was again at the window, where she wrote: *Those men who are false to those they love have a hell set aside solely for their kind. In it, they must stab themselves for a glimpse of beauty, at which they expire and wake, left only to stab themselves again.* With a smile, she closed the book and locked it in her desk. Then she ran nimbly to the door and down the stairs, throwing a light shawl about her slender shoulders, for the wind then came often and without warning from the north.

A Fortune

Once, a man went to a fortune-teller to have his fortune told. He went through his city to the district where such business is conducted. He crossed a small court-yard, and was admitted to her private chamber. She said, "You will die in the spring of the year, and cry-ing of gulls will muffle voices that may come through the wall from another room." The man was undone. He begged of her to tell him what year it would be, yet she refused. Finally, he asked, "Is fortune-telling true? Have you told me the truth? Or do lies make your fortune?" To this she replied, "It is not not-true. And when I lie, it is because a fortune is too grim to be told, and then it itself bears the burden of the lie."

Thus, in the spring of each year, the man laid out his best clothing, and went about as though bereaved, and each summer, he sang and spent great sums of money, as if to do so was nothing and of no consequence.

A Man Whose

sleight of hand was so fast that even the flourished points of his tricks could not be seen. He would pull coins from behind people's ears, but the audience would see neither the hand as it hid the coin, nor the hand as it took the coin away. His art was too great. The best of his tricks, to circle the globe in less than a second, impressed no one, as he, for reasons of his own, would always end up precisely where he had been standing before. "He's a fraud!" they chanted. And they were right, in a way. Someone else would have had to come along and teach the audience to see, before they could ever appreciate this dancing of a human hand upon a second hand.

A Gift

A heavy wooden staff is presented as a gift. In 7 of 9 possible worlds, it is a stern staff, some length of thickly carved wood, a strength to the traveler. In the 8th world, separate, it acts and speaks upon its own, casting a moving shadow, bending its long neck beneath a canopy of leaves. We may not name it there, for there it names itself. And in the 9th, that farthest of far places? Questions of the 9th remain unanswered, for statement there is nothing but swiftness of motion.

The Carriage Driver

In the midst of a terrible storm, a carriage comes thundering down a narrow drive, and pulls up at the entrance to a large mansion. The carriage doors are thrown open and a man with a haughty, powerful bearing exits the carriage and goes to the house. Hours pass. The storm is a brutal call from an angry host, and the tree line flails upon the near hills; the mud churns, pounded by the water's ceaseless assault. Still the carriage driver waits, trembling. He wants to rub the horses with a soft blanket, but he cannot, for the mud about their hooves is too deep now for him to stand in. In fact, the carriage has now sunk so that only half of its wheels rise out of the mud. The horses are curiously dead, slumped in their harness, unmoving. Soon the mud will cover them. Then and only then will he knock upon the house's great door. He will not speak when the door is answered, but will simply point, dumbfounded, at the carriage as it sinks from sight.

Three Visitors

It happened that a man returned from his day's labor to find three young women living in his house. The first was black-haired, the second yellow-haired, and the hair of the third was scarlet. They gave him different reasons for their arrival. The first said they had been drowned in a lake by their father, who could not bear their taking lovers, and this is where they had emerged. The second said they were tinkers, and had come to fix his pots. The third said they were commissioned by a lord to find the only honest man in Christendom. The beauty of but one of these girls would have lit the rooms of his house as by some small descended sun. The presence of three was uncanny and hardly to be borne. "I think you have come to take a husband," said the man. And the girls laughed, and it was true that one would remain. But which? Each day, the three would tell stories, and he would guess at who was lying. And always he would catch the black-haired girl, while the others could deceive him. For her lies were grand, implausible affairs, and a signal delight. The girls slept in his bed, all three, while he laid out a mat on the kitchen floor, and wrapped himself in a single woolen blanket. Each night he would hear their murmuring, as they composed the next day's lies. Finally, he took to writing these lies down in a leather book. For one year they stayed, and when they left all three left together, in the night. And when he looked at the book he had kept, he saw that he had only ever written down the tales the black-haired girl had told. He saw also, that he had been wrong, and that some tales he had thought false, now seemed true. A book, he thought to himself, a book of lies and truths. All equally redeeming, all damning, all brought upon us by these ghosts, our selves, and where we walk, where we have walked, where we will walk yet, guided by a chorus whose nature must always be hidden.

+ + + +

A Measure

And therefore, simply keep a cup, dusted lightly with poison, within your cupboard. When the time comes, let your fellow pour the drink, first in your cup, then in his. Drink well and long to various healths. The health of life. The health of love. And the health of hate. By then, he will be beyond help, or health, and you may say what you like for as long as you like, as well or as poorly as you know how.

picnic in ten years' time

2004

composed of:
BESTIARY nos. 1–17
and
LATER MANUAL

If, in a crowd of thousands there is preserved one who knows me, then I go free.

1

Bestiary nos. 1–17

The first dream in which I had the sensation of my true situation while asleep occurs in the 207th night; the second in the 214th.

Hervey de Saint-Denys, 1867

It Was a Later Century

I woke in the midst of a deep sleep,
some sleep such as comes over
the entirety of the world, that lasts
an infinite and indefinite period;
that, when finished, is scarcely marked

by those who slept. Out in the world
things were quiet. I went to the house
of the girl I love. She was asleep.
I dressed her, and took her with me
over my shoulder. By the river I picked

cornflowers. It was a glorious day.
From a great distance I saw a picnic,
a party of revelers, a dog. But so far,
would we ever reach them?
My girl did not answer, but looked

lovely I may tell you, in blue cotton.
I began to cross the plain.
If the day stays still we may
yet reach the other side,
to picnic there in ten years' time.

Arravelli's "View of Loum," 1542.

There are three walking by the small river,
dividing the world's belongings
into three. A hatted man in a road-stained cloak.
To the left, a miller bent upon a stick, who seems,

though crippled, to ask no help of his daughter,
she who wanders there
in the composition, the daylight rolled up
like a map against her scarlet hair.

They have been talking some time it seems
without passing beyond that row of hills
the young traveler would have crossed to come
to this crisis, to this dwelling place.

And yes, there is a mill, some four brushstrokes
delicately upon a distant withered lawn. Economy
constitutes this life: the daughter has but one
dress, that she wears; she has but one suitor,

soon to pass away; but one father, hateful,
gathering the plurals of sadness to himself;
one sadness, shared like bread; one world, beyond,
evoked once by the single traveler who has seen her

stark against foreshortened youth. For they grow old,
these wild daughters, bound to fathers
in grim lands. In them grief is a yellow tree, encircled
by a fence of bird-like angels. No shout will cause

this flock to rise to air. And here the light
is never strong enough for the face upon waking,
though it pools where the animals sleep,
and comes radiant at night through unreachable

fields, through windows which, seen with closed
    eyes,
confirm all dread—elsewhere there is a dance
that many have joined. She winces, and her one hand
is joined by the other, as if it were the painter
    himself, who,

painting an arm to hold the arm which looked
so hard to bear, had given himself away.
He *was* this traveler, Arravelli, who lied and yet did
    not lie,
a young man who said he would return.

The Privileged Girl Speaks

Whatever you do by the margin,
don't touch the tree line. It's poisonous.
Grandfather planted it sixty years ago
to keep things out. He's the only one
it cares for. You should see
the old man take a walk. He goes along
the forest edge, whistling, "St. Pierre is Home"
and it opens like a door
into some other wooden room.

Bestiary 1

It was a gray sun that stood at the door that day
and asked me for some water. Deny the sun
a cup of water? I could not.

And let me tell you something else. If it had asked
for a bed I'd have given it a bed. If it had asked
for a roasted calf, I'd have given it a roasted calf.

Soon after it left, I felt empty. I went
back to my needlepoint—three yellow bees
trying to escape from the Archangel Gabriel.

They'd stung him rather badly
on his hands and on the loose and careless
portions of his wings.

A Set Piece
to be told at gatherings

The resignation of the sheriff left nothing to be done.
The populace of that tiny hamlet poured out into
the cramped streets, half-dressed and quarrelsome.
Shops were broken into. Women were vigorously
affronted. Men too were affronted, with equal
vigor and panache. Many living near the municipal
zoo were beaten by a crowd of contrary children.
I taught everyone a hymn I had written, complete
with musical accompaniment. It went:

Kill us if you like,
but you won't like Hell
when you do (when you do)
come to (come to)
in the heat (in the hot)
in the hot (in the heat)
in the goddamn fire of the Lord.

I pretend now to have made it up, but actually an
old woman sang it to me when I menaced her
husband with my little knife. I wanted their clothing,
particularly her aubergine housecoat.

But don't be concerned for me. This sort of thing
is what everyone does when everyone does it. And
everyone who doesn't does play along, or at least
watches from the wings as those who do do what
they do, whether well or wantonly.

In another hour, we shall burn the town to bits. I've
always wanted to, and now we're in cahoots. It's a
wonderful thing, being in cahoots. One can't help
but prefer it. We'll all sit on the hill outside of town
and laugh and hold hands with pretty girls and boys
while pretty girls and boys laugh and hold hands
with us.

And the sky will stream fitfully across the sky, its
sails filled by the same wind that prompted us this

morning when we rose, rosy cheeked and ham-
handed from our all-too-narrow beds, filled with
the same rippling restless pleasure that even now
sits like a lantern in my youthful throat.

Bestiary 2

A ninety-five-year-old pilgrim is at the door.
She's knocked three times. Each time
she knocks, a knuckle in her hand breaks.
She wants a cup of water.

The desert here is wide.
In fact, this is the widest point.
Sometimes I like to go up to the roof
and ring our huge bell.
The sound floats in the air
like some hundred ships
all tossed on a single wave.
It moves out across the sand,
and nothing stops it. I think it can
go forever. I think of places the sound
goes. Cottages, little green
hedgerows, gardeners looking up.
"Oh, it's time for lunch," they must say,
"there's the bell."

A Turn

So many people had come by asking for water that
   day
that I took the last one with me to the well.
We both climbed in. It is, you know, one of my
favorite places.

At the bottom, I have set up a fine little room
with soft cushions and a phonograph.

"What would you like to hear," I ask her.

She says, "Mozart, I guess," and darts
her little tongue at me, coyly disengages a dress
   strap.

"Oh you deipnosophists are all alike!" I shout,
and put on Brahms to spite her.

In response, she wags her tail. It is long and soft,
most alluring. Alluring, one might say,
if one lived in a house in the desert.

Who knew, I ask you, who knew when I was a child
that I would one day be made a present
of such a lovely girl as this?

That Season

That season there were comedies in every playhouse.
One drought had followed another until certain
    countries
relied solely upon humor to survive their harsh
    winters.
At the time I had just begun an illustrious career
as a trainer of soldiers. I didn't further the war—it
    was

against my interest. But I taught one skill to the
    troops:
how to stand immediately behind their opponents.
A fight would start. The enemy would lunge,
and there I would be, standing behind him,
from where I might do what I liked to help or hinder

his passage through the war. The trick, of course,
was in a particular grin and a twisting of the limbs
which accompanies the sudden shift right or left.
The whole thing was rather funny, or so I thought,
as the enemy was employing experts to accomplish

precisely the same gain. The upshot? A battle
in which two armies twirled around like dancers
in some avant-garde ballet. Everyone came out
to the countryside to watch. It was the start
of a short but bloodless epoch in world history.

Bestiary 3

And then one day the pilgrimage route changed. No one wanted to see the pillar in the desert, and so I had no more visitors. It was sad really, or so I thought at first. But then I went back to the history book I was writing.

Such a book . . .

It doesn't even use our verbs. They're too pointed. Only causeless words

can please, a record without
a point of view. History proper,
for the first time.

Every physical change
in the world listed, along with its place.

I can work only at night, while I'm asleep.
Dreaming, one has time for such things.

Nonetheless, I fall behind. If only I had
an assistant, a really clever one . . .

All hermits begin by pretending to be hermits.
And by liking birds.

First Verse

In the house of my sleeping eye the veins of wood
run from the furniture down into the floor.

When I lay my hands upon the table's surface
the entire feathered expanse

shifts in flight.

Parades

And when you are finally caught and questioned,
it is discovered, sadly, that you know
nothing of use. Your captors exchange glances,
     nod.
You are released in the freedom of some afternoon,

some autumn of the year, your coat, hat, returned
as if to continue your life. Now it is you

in the world again. In yellowing rooms, life
becomes no more than the places where it occurs.
At the pier in darkness, parades will cross the water,
visible but once. Or I could say

I saw the wind coming hard along the river
touching all it passed.

How are things consequent? When they catch you
again, what will you say? That all things
may be weighed, may be raised and weighed
by two human hands?

A Calico Ascription

I stand by the pump with a deaf girl.
She is on the verge of a breakthrough.
I am very earnest and sedulous.
I am possibly the best teacher
who has ever lived. I lever the pump's
arm, and water begins to flow.

Meanwhile, in my days as a
snake-charmer, a great painter
is sketching me. He's on holiday
and has inserted a slight grin
onto this quiet face.
I wasn't grinning. You mustn't
suppose I was grinning.

I've always known day by day
my real work approaches.
Not for anything would I grin,
not even once.
The work means too much.

Our Plots, Our Comfort

By an old mill my father is waiting
with hundreds of other fathers.

I would like for them to keep
each other company,

but from here it is plain —
none of them is speaking.

What's that in his hand?
An old leather wallet.

He's taking something out of it,
a picture, I wonder of whom.

Who next will go to join him,

walking long there
in the early places of my life?

Report from Our Lands

Nevertheless the war continued
trembling the cupboards
where we slept, cracking the long
stone walkways of the village, as
if there were no other way to act

successfully in this foolish place,
as if were we in its place, this war,
we had no light but brute gleaming.

Bestiary 4

A race of men who can turn themselves into not
    animals
but inanimate objects. Europeans reach this tribe
by boat. What a grand city, they say. What fine broad
avenues, such as you might see in Paris. How lovely
the women in their long satin dresses, with their
fans and shuddering hair. Much feasting goes on.

Days later, the discovery is made. Orders are sent
    back
across the sea to be confirmed by the Queen.
Orders are confirmed. The populace is brought
    out
into a series of aesthetically ideal city squares
and forced at gunpoint to change directly
into gold. They object at first, then the King

changes himself into a large gold vase. His sons
become a pair of gold grates (for a confessional).
    Their
children become lockets. The royal servants
take the form of forks and spoons. This is general

throughout the population, and the objects
become a sort of faux-history, where each object

fails in its attempt to mimic the life lived.
Historians today wonder if this was intentional.

Bestiary 5

These pregnant methods, cheerful
and fat, leaning from filthy casements
in the side of June may yield
ink-eyed marionettes so lovely

that their gestures,
pointedly describing strings,
mean little even to the adept.

Mary. Isa. Joan. Celeste.
Roaming the grounds
of this quartered preserve.
Mary lays a lacquered hand

upon your cheek. Joan's plain head
inclines—she is speaking
but the voice is from above.

Isa crouches in the near future;
she will scream at a painted boar
that bursts from a stand of trees.
Celeste is absent. Or is Joan

speaking of her when she says,
"I knew a matchstick once
that burned like the hands of a clock."

From the scenery then, a wooden creaking
as of someone's descent. Applause.
Applause. And in the front row
a man's heart bursts in his chest.

EAST RIDING

ONE

The forest was much larger than anyone had previously
   thought.

So large that one couldn't find one's way back.

Luckily there were many lovely clearings and crisp glo-
   rious mornings.

It was therefore possible to live.

Also there were rose bushes everywhere, each larger
   than the one before

(and how we loved to discover the roses, naming them
   after ourselves).

And biplanes would pass overhead.

TWO

In the period before I entered the forest, I thought
that there was the world, one small corner of which
was the forest. Now it has become clear to me —
there is the forest, and the world is but
one small corner of it, exceedingly small, humble even.

For I have seen them meet in the street, and I can tell
    you
it is the world that makes the deeper bow, the world
that goes away, hat in hand, making furtive glances back
to see if the forest has turned also to look. Which never
    happens.

And furthermore, one can't find one's way back.
Luckily there are many lovely clearings and crisp glori-
    ous mornings.

THREE

On one such morning I went out looking
for the clearest of seven streams. Seven there were,
running through the forest, and all of them clear.
Which was the clearest?

I put my hand in the first stream.
My hand turned the color of the night sky, which is
    mottled.
This distressed me, so I put my hand in my pocket.
On to the next stream.

I put my other hand in the second stream.
It soon began to move of its own accord.
This distressed me further. With a stern act of will
I put it too in my pocket.
On again.

At the third stream, a man was standing.
Both of his hands were stuck in his pockets also.

"What do you suppose we do next?" he asked.

FOUR

The forest is different than was supposed.
It is darker in the trees, lighter between them.

Passing between them is its own skill,
separate from the skill of being in clearings.

This is how it goes: you wander for years
in the world, then you find the edge of the forest.

You enter, and wander for days in the forest.
You try to find your way back.

Instead you find a clearing. Also you find out
whether or not you can live alone in the forest.

Many can't. Others come after, and bury them.
Hungry little roses grow then from the ground.

FIVE

We of the forest wonder often about the biplanes.
From where do they take off?
Where do they land?

It should be easy to answer this question,
as there are so many of us asking it and spending time
wondering and musing.

The trouble is, only one person ever saw the biplanes.
He mentioned it in passing. Afterwards,
he refused to speak of it. Otherwise, he was silent.

If you happen to see a biplane, you'd tell me, wouldn't
    you?
one of my friends asked me.

Of course I would, I say. But I'm not sure of it.
I'm not sure I wouldn't follow the plane alone to the land-
    ing field
(which must be a clearing deeper in the forest)
there to make friends with the aviators, and beg them
    to take me in.

Such a life it would be to fly in the air above the forest!
Distinctly I feel above the forest, luckily it is always
    gloriously morning.
And in a plane, one can easily find one's way,

though not, of course, back to the world. One could,
I mean, find one's way deeper into the forest.

SIX

What can I tell you about the forest
that you can't read in books? Well,
our lives here are bared like the trunks of trees.
We believe fundamentally in things that are
quite obviously not true. On such things
our happiness is often based.

For instance, the allegiance of friends.
We of the forest are known cowards.
We make free with each other's possession,
make love to each other's husbands and wives.

At first it is odd, I know.

Pierre for instance, has a gorgeous wife.
She wears a little dress of leaves. People are forever
pulling at it as she curtsies by on her girlish legs.
One day she asked me if I would like
to go and find the Monumental Rose.

Where is it? I asked.
Deeper in, she said. We really must be going.

And so we went. I took Pierre's name.
He took mine. We shook hands.

Have a fine time, he said. Be good.
The forest is much larger than you think.

THEN—a rustling of leaves. Cora had gone.
I'd better go, I said, following into the rustling
through the glorious light.

SEVEN

The philosophers who end up in the forest
stop writing books and begin instead
trying to grow herb-gardens. Every time
it happens the same way. It's so funny.
There's Spinoza. What's he doing? Pruning oregano.
There's William James.

What are you doing, William James? I inquire.
But he doesn't answer, so absorbed is he
in laying string for vines. I watch for a minute,
standing fast by his elbow, intent on his progress.
Before you go, he says absently,
be sure to take a sprig of parsley for your buttonhole.

This I do. Need I say it twice?
We of the forest are terribly dashing.

EIGHT

Everyone in the forest has the same dream every night.
We sleep and are immediately awake again
in a tiny one-room house. There is a storm
in the out-of-doors. It is clear to everyone
that it is the biggest storm there's ever been.
The forest, in fact, has been flattened.

All of a sudden, the storm halts.
We rush out of the cottage door
and are standing in the middle of a clearing
that stretches infinitely in every direction.

It's then we realize that the forest
has not been flattened. Nor was there
a storm. Merely that
this is a deeper clearing, one we may
someday find. We wake then, invigorated,
and without so much as a by-your-leave,
rush off into the dew-strewn underbrush.

NINE

East Riding. It is the name that the world has
for the forest. I recall I was a child when I
heard it first. Still, I felt drawn.

I would go sometimes to the highest part
of the farm country and gaze eastward to the sea
of treetops drowsing in the distance,
hazy day, the sun's rays mingling with the dust
and hanging in the air like the passing of hands.

I believe, I told the village priest, in East Riding.
Dismayed, he spoke with my parents,
counseling them to send me to the part of the world
farthest from East Riding.
But my father laughed. I recall this vividly.
He laughed at the priest, and raised me up
eye level into the air. He said,

"I believe you are going to East Riding.
Already you've left us."

He took my mother's hand and stood in the doorway
looking off into the distance as though watching
the progress of some traveler on a distant road.

But I was still in the house. My things weren't even
    packed.
The priest stuck his sharp elbow in my ribs.

See? he said. So I slipped between my parent's legs
and walked and walked and walked.

When I reached the distant road, I could see
that they were watching. I waved. They waved back.

And I followed the road where it went
beneath a canopy of trees.

TEN

On the deeper paths, one can't know
for sure if one is welcome, save by clearings.
If one encounters lovely clearings
and crisp glorious mornings, then one has
cannily chosen the right path.

At other times it's as dark as the inside
of a leaded window on an old cloudy block.
No one visits anymore, and the oldest man
is older by far than the histories he tells.
This is his defense, and it's a keen one.

So I know to turn back, sometimes.
Always, it's then one is given a small but kind
clearing to sleep in, and a tiny rose in greeting.

Be thou pleased by the day, and by waking
to light. From the bottom of a well

comes the vaguest song, but it is, I think,
known to you, muttered in your aging heart.

For if we all do not know a thing,
then no one can know it. It is not given us
to have that which is not instinctively

present in the world. On the softest grass
imaginable, I lay my head. It is quiet
and the path has been lost.

The path, I say, has been lost.
It is lovely to say things in a human voice
and hear in your mind or in the air,

and hear in the forest a human reply.

Grimoir *or* the hole beside the millstream

Little Teag was sleeping on a bed of moss. Just
then up crept a satyr, the cruelest, most straying,
canceling satyr of them all. He stripped poor Teag
down to the bone with his sharp teeth and left
the little skeleton for someone else to find. Such a
delicate skeleton. I came upon it while walking. I
pointed to it with my hand, and went to it with my
feet. John Spence, who was along, did not come
closer. He said it wasn't a proper burial. I said we
should give it one. And so we had my little sister

out with us next day dressed up in ribbons and lace, and I wore my high collar and Spence had a good cap. We wrapped the little fellow in a clean sheet of linen and brought him down to a hole we'd dug by the millstream. I said a few words then, like a deacon, I said, "IF it was a satyr that did this, or a lamb, neither will I worship. Braver than the soil is the flesh that lends it breadth." And through the woods then the satyr came, galloping on its hind legs. We hid in the grave 'til it had gone, and only then emerged to lay upon the ground in the groggy afternoon, listening to the brook. Before we left I filled the hole, spreading the earth flat enough for any boy to walk upon. John Spence marked it with a stone, in case we should ever again need a hiding place in that part of the forest.

Casuist's Aside

And being wrong about the colors

light takes
in the eyes of my animals,

I wonder now what many failures
of difference I have made,

trying to map the catchments
of other lives

with brown scenes from this single self.

Missive in an Icelandic Room

> RITA KEPT LAZARUS IN A CHINESE BOX
> & FED HIM PEPPERMINTS UNTIL HE NO
> LONGER KNEW WHO OR WHAT HE WAS.
> THEN SHE GAVE HIM A PAPER CROWN
> AND A JAR WITH A TADPOLE AND BADE
> HIM SIT BESIDE HER.

And If They Should Tell You

That I have debauched the youth of this town. That
    further, I,
a youth of this town, have been

debauched, have helped in the debauching of others.
    Have helped
myself in and to the debauching

of the others, well . . . I would not be overly troubled at
    the news.
For you see, I have a new

project in mind. Imagine a house, a shack rather, in
    some flyspeck
town. Within the house, a trap door.

And beneath the door, an entire realm of wickedness!
He who first spoke of it

has promised we will meet there, and I must confess, I
    look now
often at the map he left,

look often upon those impressions his thin and supple
    fingers
made in oily remark.

Missive in an Icelandic Room 2

Harangued
by the ring
master, the
paper circus
fell to
muttering.
Johan wrung
his hand
and stroked
the elephant's
thick skin.
"How will

we fathom
the mind of
the audience,
if we cannot
name it truly
our oldest
and deepest
foe?"

The First Mime

A young king is unhappy. He takes
to going out with a false beard,
sackcloth robes, a long knife, a leather bag.
He soon becomes known about town in this capacity,
and liked. He takes a mistress. He spends time
in common taverns, in playhouses.
No one knows his secret, save a palace guard
his own age, who lets him out of the castle each
     night.

One night the disguised king
returns to the castle, only to find the guard,
now also disguised, ruling from his throne.
Before the King can speak, the new King orders him
     seized
by palace guards who cut out his tongue
and cart him away to a nearby asylum.
He is heard from no more.

The new King despises his children
and has them strangled. On the other hand,
he takes great pleasure in his association with the
    Queen,
who has guessed nothing.

One day it is announced before the court
that a madman is at the gates, claiming to be the
    King.
The King grants him an audience, at which time
the madman tells the court the story
that you have just been told, this time

through a series of hand gestures. Naturally,
no one is convinced. The King, however,
takes pity on the man, and allows him
to take up service as his jester, in which capacity,
I may happily relate, the man excels.

Word of the mute jester spreads,
and soon the court of this King is spoken of
throughout many lands
as a place of enlightenment and culture.

Version

She wanted desperately to know
what was in the green box.

A green box on a coarse black cloth
in a burnished-gold room.

She leaned in close,
her soft hair falling across
both our faces.

If only, she breathed,
I could dream my way
into that citadel

and wake, the green box
clutched in my hands.

Antonym of My Name

It was a dull play about a boy whose pet calf was being
    slaughtered.
Apparently no one could stop this thing from happening.
The butcher was played by a florid man with a huge beard.

Somehow having a beard made him likely to kill a calf.
I felt sorry for the calf, which was an actual calf,
and must have been on sedatives. It let everyone drag
    it around

on a little tether of worn rope. I wanted to write a review
for a major newspaper saying, "the little sedated calf
stole the show in Sunday's performance of *Johan's Gift*."

Instead, two hours into the performance, the boy has his feeble
arms wrapped around the calf which isn't breathing.
Someone is singing a lullaby, trying to make him fall asleep

so they can take the animal to the block. The butcher
has a surprisingly sweet voice. Nine tawdry little urchins
dressed in sparkly tutus do a dance around the boy.
   This is his dream

beginning. Each boy has a sedated calf in his arms.
The butcher sneaks in the window and is reaching for the calf
when the dream-urchins draw swords and stab him to death.

They were just pretending to be dream-urchins. HA!

Missive in an Icelandic Room 3

Clever remarks were no good,
Elizabeth realized. A sparrow was a sparrow,
and would never be a proper friend,

nor make up for the legions
of her childhood who'd abandoned her,
and left her to drift in this half-haze,
this country holiday without end.

And that there is

at the core of all the great artists, all the great thinkers, some severe misunderstanding, arrived at in childhood and never disclosed, never brought to light. Such a generative force propels imagination, skews thought, forces realization. And since it is, at heart, a mistaken conception, buried deep in the artist's past, one cannot hope to emulate that mind's growth, nor even to find out what it was about which that child was wrong.

In a Glass Coffin Beneath Alexandria, in Alexander's Dusty Skull, One Image Still Trembling

Darius, in a beggar's filthy robe, passing
in the street below, a guard of six
beggars about him.

A faint frustration
like a candle's negligible smoke:

Alexander's many thousand troops seized
all the beggars of Issus.
But none was Darius.

Bestiary 8

I am watching a girl draw in her notebook.
She draws a little broad-shouldered fellow
with big eyes. Beneath it she writes,

"A WORM BORES INTO FYODOR's BRAIN."

Then she draws the worm. As she says,
it is indeed boring into his brain.
In no time the little chap will be insensible.

While there's still a moment left, I intercede
on Fyodor's behalf. "At least put a doctor
on the scene. At least that."

She draws a doctor on a corner of the paper.
He is wearing pajamas.
"I had to get him out of bed," she says. "He hates that."

In the cafe, men are playing at cards,
smoking and drinking. A large moon has risen
over the cantina wall. In every direction,

the world is rising out of itself, stretching
like a healed animal. And I too am part of this.
Rising, I say to the girl, "Let's go to the lake."

Bestiary 9

Up she gets. Her things go into a cloth bag.
No one notices us leave except a yellow cur that follows
    us
for miles across the filthy blackened landscape.

Not This But The Truth

A YOUNG WOMAN IS AT THE DOOR. SHE
    ENTERS,
CROSSES THE ROOM AND OPENS A LOCKED
    BOX.
INSIDE IS THE POET, JESSE BALL, CURLED
    UP ASLEEP.
SHE RUNS HER HAND THROUGH HIS HAIR
    SLOWLY,
CAREFUL NOT TO WAKE HIM, FOR IF HE
    SHOULD WAKE,
SHE MURMURS SOFTLY, THEN WHAT WOULD
BECOME OF ALL OUR SECRET AND
    IMPLAUSIBLE HOPES?

Bestiary 10

The sadness of colored glass bottles stands in rows
in the disused pharmacy.

I went there once
thinking to play a trick. Oh what a trick.

Two Dogs

As if these true books were given up
in guttural jest,
in flawed and flawing laughter—

And how, upon the road this day
at a line of shadowed yards two dogs
turned their heads and beheld me.

Could I but have called to them by name

we might have gone on, saying,
Evening crouches like a banister,
our famed poverty the steps beneath.

A Bargain

A trail of clothespins held my dress on
as I wandered in the wilderness.

I wandered for seven years
and each year I grew immeasurably
more beautiful.

How many, I ask you, how many
lives can there be that pass
without a glance to right or left?

I made a bargain with a mill-stone.
I said, "Be my lover."
And it replied,
"Better you had died."

And in the Hollow Tree There Was a Note That Said:

Not Satan, but some other
more shrewd impresario
created Music with a cunning
beyond good, beyond evil.
Therefore Music, like certain
other human tongues,
is not a source but a mutiny.

Bestiary 13

My mother lives by the smallest road
you could possibly imagine. She walks up it

each day, and down. I think sometimes
that such a road changes our possibilities.

By this I mean, you will never see this road
because I will never tell you

where to find my mother.

Forty-Year Soliloquy

Was there a way we were taught
to talk in doorways? Occasions,
I have always felt, should be the guide

to best propriety: a form for speech
while walking; a way to converse
surprised; a method for

engaging someone whom
you have embarrassed. These
and others would be part

of that manual I wish I had created
forty years back. Forty years
might be time enough, if the work

had been addressed by all,
for those now living to know
how to speak not just their minds

but also what they hope.

A Setting

At the Ambassador's house the women took up
precisely half the space they ought to have
in order to be pleasing to the eye,
and everyone said savage things to each other,
in hopes they would be overheard.

But I was not amused. Consider this:
My cat had passed away just hours before
on a little plot of grass in the front yard.
In fact, I was carrying it over my shoulder

in a sagging gray canvas bag. And there I was,
there, there, there, as if anything could be solved
by foolish scripted action or the eyes that follow it.

Bestiary 14

Before he left, he passed me the knife
and I used it to cut my bonds.

It was a very dull knife
and the cutting took years.

Guards would wager on my progress.
"Sooner or later," they'd say,

while washing the changing fashions
out of their thin and cunningly braided hair.

Bestiary 15

Her picture came to when I threw the water
over. Its eyes began to follow me.

No notion I had then, such as is in me now —
what it can mean to wake a thing that's past.

Bestiary 16

Cardinal Piccate, famed priest-turned-skeptic of the
    15th century:

we are somehow present at his denunciation. The pope
declares the excommunication to a crowd of hundreds
who have gathered in the papal gardens. A peculiar hand
    gesture
accompanies the statement. This gesture is much imitated
later that day and in the days to follow. Would that I could
    say
it was just the opening of a hand, or a gathering
of fingertips *this way.* No, you must observe it for yourself,
or read Cartoccio's treatise on the matter. Later popes

resigned themselves to its loss as a tool of governance, so
    difficult

was it to master. But even now the sentence is being
    repeated.

Piccate, with his braided beard, his sun-scalded brow, is
    led off in chains.
Unbeknownst to the guards, you and I follow to his estate
on the hills outside Rome. He is put inside the main
    building,
with all his household and all its attendant creatures.
Hoisted above this building on scaffolding huge caul-
    drons tip
inevitably sealing the house in four-foot-thick
impenetrable hot wax. This was apparently

common practice. Skeptical thought must be dealt with

entirely or not at all, so says the Manual of Kings
and we who would rule must learn their fluid lessons.
To that end there is preserved, in a vault beneath the
    Vatican,
the house-entire of Cardinal Piccate, still sealed,
    hermetically,
poised in its last obdurate skepticism, caught beneath
    a lens
broad as a careful century.

The view from outside is stunning,
Cartoccio wrote, though it can in no way be compared

to that view achieved from the inaccessible interior.

Bestiary 17

A boundary. Laughter in the spanning rooms
I am forced to attend, one by one.

How attached they are, these unlikely places

one to another, street to gateway,

gateway to stair, stair to corridor
and from there — hidden rooms

and cluttered portals.
They say, *I sang a song and you were in it*

but you left just as I began. How I believe them.

It is a terribly hot summer
and from beneath this shading tree

there is a song just faintly, prompted

by my heel, each factored place singing out
when I have crossed some bordering veil.

But now I have my hearing,

and a group of men come into view,
walking with the theater, livelihood and jest.

Theirs was the tune I heard. Never to belong

to me, save in swayed refrain, or in the manner
of a berth laid by, as it was spoken to me

by the grand ship incidence, that said,

This is the tunnel through which the water flows
and I will bear you as water is borne: in a bucket, in a pan,

or loose throughout the drowning sea.

Missive From a Room in Pau

A slightly pale tinge to the day,
as if even now it were being remembered.

Asking Advice of the Scissors,
in their Small Drawer

By way of introduction, I use a soft white handkerchief
to polish the lens of my spyglass.

Afterwards we spy on your enemies.

Shall we attack them one by one
in the supposed safety of their beds?

Missive In a Room in Pau

A child on an invisible donkey demands your attention,
but you go right past him during an autumn day
one hundred years from now.

I appear at times

I appear at times to children when they go alone too
    long,
saying—sister, brother, how has it been with you? Dim
    forests,

balked women, these have sown signposts, not children
upon the broad aisles. For it is in belief that our progress
has long been halted. Tell me, what momentum stirs us
but truth and avoidance. Oh, long night's approach
upon a warning. Long day, day all through afternoon
and the men who watch beneath the wooden shelters!
    I say
go to them, speak there, speak your fill. But then — how
    little

there is to say. I demand of you, the things you thought
    last night.
Tell us, you must tell us. You must tell us and grow old.

Missive In a Room in Pau

I saw you on that windy day when you were
as yet of no account, roaming the streets in a borrowed
    coat,
practicing the deft touch, the brief smile, and the slight
    collision
that are THE PICKPOCKET's FEW FRIENDS.

Missive From a Room in Pau

The town was so small you could only glance at it out
    the window of a moving train.

Here is some information about turtles:

The Corinthian Ambulant Turtle is named for its tri-partite crown, a growth of horn to which scientists are troubled to ascribe utility. The Corinthian is the larg-est of the box turtles, being an incredible five feet in length, from tip of rear claw to sharp forebeak. It is noted for its dissimilarity to much of placid turtlekind. In nature it is perhaps closest to the brutal snapping turtles of North America, which are quite capable of snapping a small branch in two, particularly if that branch is being poked at them by an unctuous child. The Corinthian subsists upon a diet of Vruvkii nuts from the Vruvkii tree. These grow on the slopes of the Limbok Mountains east of the Urals. It is difficult to say whether it is the fault of the Vruvkii tree or the Corinthian Ambulant that neither have spread across foreign geographies. Certainly should one do so, the other would follow. The tree cannot spread, for its seed is carried within the nigh impenetrable Vruvkii nuts. And the turtle cannot spread, for on what would it subsist, were it to pass beyond its precious orchards of Vruvkii? In scientific tests, Russian researchers have managed to break the nuts, but it required the persis-tent use of a steam drill. Only the irresistible jaws of the Corinthian Ambulant Turtle can break the nut clean as by a whim and, digesting the tender nut, release the Vruvkii seed into the soil along with its own fecal matter. In terms of literary and historical significance, the Corinthian Ambulant has known both. Tolstoy's *Anna Karenina* is menaced by one of these beasts while out picnicking as a child. And none other than the famous Rasputin was known to keep one at his side at all times. That turtle, nicknamed Levkar Klevar, meaning, Head Lost in the Clouds, can be seen in pictures from the period. Canning's *Momentary History of the Occident's Orient* includes a passage devoted purely to this marvelous beast:

> It was with trepidation, then, that I stretched out my gloved hand to pet the thing. For had it not that same day snapped the Countess M.'s arm off at the elbow? The priest assured me there would be no repetition of such untowardity. I can report that its crown is quite hard. Were I not gloved I might have scratched the skin of my fingers on one of the many jagged edges that press forth. Though I cannot agree with Rasputin that it, rather than the lion, is king of beasts, I can say with some authority, it is certainly a king, though of what, I know not.

Inventions

Some having posited a lion, others must posit the lion
    having victims.
These victims in turn must posit things, things that are
    lost within the lion's
    grim and enfolding city, that belly-land of growth
and indolence.

100th verse

For though I think that what we are
we are not long or sour: grosvenor,
selah, or a game of chance; it is
soon said: lay me at your feet as if
to bid the world with its own name.
What name could that be? Who,
tearer of the dog sinew that contracts
vowels, could force a stated name
as mantle to the world? Enforce a name?
It would be easier to bear a prophet
from between pale legs. There are not
many prophets, nor many right names.
And in the air a sky is forming.

A Scolding

And so you see, my little jars of marmalade, there's trouble
    enough in the district,
and trouble enough in your heads without you going
    rambling about the shantytown,
nickels clattering, on your way to gamble with that pie-
    bald rascal, old Head-of-a-Mule!

Verse

Do I *subscribe* to that living which may be had
from faith in events? One may
persuade the ground to house vegetables,
pages to house unforgivable solutions. Really,
there are none, only names and this listening.

Hours conclude what birth begins,
not death but sympathy. Men agree
on seven things only, and six will go
undiscovered. We know vaguely
what the earth is, ourselves shapeless in a fog.

The secret signal of the greatest landed
invasion was a verse by Verlaine. Now
I sit, wondering what movements
of men may take my words to herald
deeds to which they're sent.

One may sit alone, housing hours in a cupboard
with which only this may be done,
to suppose that one may smile, and in smiling
find a damning fact — things may seem true.
Then, the sound of a key in the door —

people enter the room,
 your name unspoken in the air about
their heads. What can you say
to such people? Not you, not you —
only life can force them away.

The Distressing Effect of Rumors

I reached into the jar, and sought out their
little heads with the palm of my hand.

I could hear them talking and scuffling about.

One said:

Because of the present circumstances, we will soon
be forced to sell our children.

To that another replied:

But what of we who have no children?

Missive In a Room in Pau

—What can you do to be of use? asked the Inspector.

—I can make a noise like a bee and I can run fast around
corners, said Jana politely.

Balloon Diary, week of the pastoral revolt:

Miles of hedge, farms, fields. Beneath my hand, the til-
ler is like the soft neck of a soft necked girl when girls
come to you for the first time, not knowing who or what
they are. You tell them, and they rise like the pasture
lands as we float and flourish. I feel sometimes that I
am like a god-cloud, harboring useless intents that can-
not possibly apply to the things upon the ground. Yet
sometimes we descend, Balloon and I, to sample the
wares in a market, or touch the aged faces of the or-
phanages on southward tending prairies. As we passed
in evening above an esplanade on which satin girls ca-
vorted, touching hands and lips to satin boys, a man
came whistling along and hid in a barrel, hid his body
first and then his face. Oh my I said, I wonder . . . and
wondering, I paused the balloon as you, my friend,
might pause your finger above an item in the evening
paper. Another came soon along the narrow cliff-walk,
a bright-eyed lad in a fresh suit, with a tiny bottle of
medicine balanced upon his outstretched hand. It was

the serum meant to cure his village, afflicted to the east. This fact came later, in the guise of further suffering, when it seemed that all the suffering had been meted out. Or perhaps I lie! Perhaps it never came at all! In any case—a fine looking lad with a glass bottle, a fine looking barrel wherein waits the curiosity of the modern age. Yes, the barrel burst as past the waistcoat walked. The serum was snatched and no explanation given, but for a sliding from shadow to shadow like imagined monkeys that are not real monkeys, but seem so for a moment. The lad grasped at the barrel shards as if some intelligence might be had from them. In the bottom of the barrel he found a deck of cards, all the cards blank, save the seven of clubs. To it he gave a name: Pistol that I Forfeit. And vowing to forget his plague-ridden village, he traveled into the distant lands of Avecture and Intiman where he made a name for himself as a slayer of false doctors.

Of course, I followed the interloper in my balloon for leagues. He *was* a loper, a real long-walker of the old variety. But faced with a balloonist, well the outcome is obvious; he could not escape. With my long hooked pole I caught him up.

And if the pollywog doesn't keep her date with the pastry-chef, then the silly little waxwork owl won't hoot and wake the milk-maid and I promise, I really promise, we'll be visited by hellions in the simpering night.

The Well

A small boy lived with his grandfather in a little house on a large property. On the far back hill of the farthest corner was an old cemetery. The gravestones had been brushed by the wind and rain until they were small white markers without word or direction. The boy loved to go there, for the grass was deep and soft. And in between the gravestones it was always very quiet. And there was a well. The grandfather said it was the deepest well in the world.

++

When they dropped stones down, there never was a sound, no matter how long they waited. And in a place like that, you can wait a long time. Not even the sun could reach the bottom, not even at noon on a clear day.

++

The boy began to spend all of his time there, looking down the well. His grandfather began to worry about him. He told the boy that he was no longer allowed to go there. And one day his grandfather locked the cemetery gate with a long iron key.

++

For a week, the boy stayed away. But it seemed to him that the rest of the property, his grandfather's house, even the world of the town, was gray and shrunken. He wanted only to lie in the quiet of the cemetery and gaze down the well.

++

Days passed in the drudgery of dust caught in household sunlight. Finally it was too much for him. He stole into his grandfather's room and found the long iron key on a hook high up on the wall. He pushed a chair underneath. Climbing onto the chair, he took the key.

++

Away he went through the tall grass to the high hill and the cemetery gate. He slid the key into the lock; the gate swung open. Beyond it, the path was a clean rut through the green. In the field and by the road the world's bustling had been loud in his ears. Now in the shade of the cemetery the boy felt soothed. He lay down on a bed of moss and fell into a deep sleep.

++

In his sleep he dreamed of climbing into the well and dropping through the loose air to land softly on the bottom. A man was there. He seemed familiar. Beside him was a woman. They took the boy in their arms and their warmth was a long warmth. There was a staircase leading downwards. Its stone steps were smooth marble. He took their hands and descended the stair.

++

He woke. It was afternoon and quiet. The sun was cradling his mossy bed with a hazy slow light. He went to the well and looked down it. Old smells seemed to rise and greet his nose. He remembered the faces; he remembered what was at the bottom of the well. He felt then that he had come round to the beginning of a world that was gone.

++

Away across the landscape, the boy's grandfather ran on skinny legs, waving his arms. But the boy did not hear him. The boy was standing on the side of the well. The grandfather yelled and redoubled his pace, struggling to run through the bracken. But it was no good. Into the well the boy went. Into the well he went for good. And he fell for a very long time.

Missive from a Room in Pau

And now we have come to that last country of
    THURSDAYS and JULY.

Autoptic: 1

At five, I relented and began to speak.

For much of my life I forgot
that this might even be regretted.

Autoptic: 2

I began with the anger of friends
and gathered it beneath my coat.

It kept me warm through first
one winter, then another; I

became grateful, and so the anger went away.
I sought it again, with thin hands,

a hypnotist's assurance.
I was told do not provoke it, and I,

I listened well. I took my fists
to the glassworks where the lovers

I once became with a trumpet call
were arrayed in fine rows, two by two.

They were astonished,
they who had gone apart so long.

Come back to us, they cried, their voices
thin like old glass. *Come back, you fool.*

SO I TOOK THEM TOO beneath my coat
and called it precaution.

Autoptic: 3

I loved a man who was a scholar of war,
and I hated war, and loved it

even as I hated it. For there are places

where the dust is entertaining like a clavier
each mote abrupt like a struck and filigreed note,

there and then gone, where horsemen,
mercenary, intent on the several work of death,

gallop through books upon the table,
laying siege to centuries of imaginings,

as men in armored lines advance,
their spears like spun cloth.

Autoptic 4: House Up-Hill

I stand, gray and wan, by the stove, boiling tea, and trees
    climb down
through the winter hills to bring me news.

They whisper through the tiny window kept for just this
    reason
in long syllables that reach to my long ears.

A woman is living in a hole, they say, a hole buried in the
    ground,
and birds are fools who talk of nothing,

or little, not both. The wind is vain, and furthermore
    blind, wanting only to be thought
of in kind ways. In this

it is often gratified. Yet still, the fury. And too a boy
    wandered upon
a deep part of the wilderness. He can't come out.

He is unharmed but very sad, and you would, they say,
    you would
take pity if you saw him, such a small boy,

so sad, and hungry. He won't last more than a day. He'll
    die of
exposure, as children do in books.

He's just that way, through the trees. *That way.*

I smile at such ruses; steam rises from the kettle. Not for
    nothing
did I go once to the forest's heart, there to learn my ample
    secrets.

Belie, Belie

Belie the page upon which this pen sits
like a craven monarch whose kingdom

is as utter and as useless as his fool.

Belie the doldrums that assail
the wizened faces I once bore

in sickness as a raging child.

Belie the becoming and the knowing
of what little I might become, when set

beside that lathe, the sea, and all it does.

Belie the dastard clock, the vagrant
calendar, the leash of seasons, the stunted

grace of graveyards.

Belie the waltzes, the saddened mazurkas that infect
even the joyous as they dance.

Austromancy

And so, in the afternoon I am often

caught feeling as though I've gone missing
from the life I was to lead.

This is the chief pleasure, I tell myself,
of young poets.

I followed a Ribbon

I followed a ribbon that trailed from a hand
and it led through the grazing of crowds upon pavement,
through laities and simpering voices in evening,
past lives that might be given me in confidence
and confidences that cannot be given in life,
through the drawers of perished infants, where the bed
linens still keep the traces of tiny bodies,
and beside ladders upon which men stand
as on a willful pride that harms all those beneath,
all down, all down at last, to the harbor
where such ribbons trail the water in a hundred places.
I cannot find my own amidst so many,
but I pretend to, and taking up an oar I leap
foolhardy into a passing boat.
"Do you need an oarsman?" I call out needlessly.
As if there were anything left to do but row.

Autoptic: 7

Prussian blue, the coat
I thought to wear, but cannot,
down into the morning town.

I am a great anticipator, building
my empire with such things as
coats and colors, unexpected visits,

dogs that take their leashes in their
mouths, and gentle-eyed rascals
who follow each other

up through the limbs of trees.

Auturgy Refrain

Brown cotton, and how we have all forgotten
so much that we had promised.

Aching then where light
plays upon long floors
in the cleverest rooms of the skull,

I proceed to become
that which I have admired in
those many I admire.

Is it enough that this ambition holds
one moment? Two would be
miraculous, and three, as good as true.

I count the blemishes
that stain my good name.
But who can count so long?

A good name — what use is it
but for causing jealousy in idle hearts?

No, I was not made to bear a tool like that.

I was Awake a very long Time

Not a carnival but loud
unexplainable noise. The sound

of someone being chased.
Dogs waiting silently beneath hedges.

A man sifting flour on a park bench
no reason given.

Autoptic: 8

Grief, do me no favors. I have grown my hair long,
as you bid me. I have learned to roll
a coin below my knuckles. I have written down now

years of dreams; much of my life has passed in writing
down these books of sleep. And so you see that I can
no longer turn only to what's true

when I speak of my experience. Sainted men
wander in forests that have been set to rows.
And here, today, already I have found a stone

shaped like a day I passed in a life I can't claim as my own.
The wind calls water what it wants to call it and passes
overhead. But water names wind from within,

as storms proceed in hinges, all through the captive
captive, captivated light. Therefore, I show my face boldly
in a portrait of my great-great-grandfather. In reply

a deep breath in my lungs, and the room about me
actual as nothing can be actual. My hand is badly cut,
and I cannot say how long it has been bleeding.

And yes, I'm sorry, but that hardly matters now.

Speech in a Meadow

Leopold and his benefactor pause beside a hill on the
    benefactor's estate. In the hill
there is a door. The day is cold, and bright.

IT WAS this door, years ago, you understand,
that prompted me to begin a wayward life.

Behind it I imagined a tidy room, a hearth,
some bespectacled, bewhiskered creature, conversant

with the courtesies of our times. Strange, but with
things to tell me. You understand.

Later I thought it to be a long and lamplit hall.

And lately I've imagined my portrait hanging there,
quietly, as the lamps are covered,

one by one. The angriest man I ever saw
broke his own teeth with a hammer. For as he said,

It's dark as night inside the sun,
and that is where we're told to wait. But this

was years ago. I imagine things are different now.

Yet still no answer from the Captain,
not yet, young Leopold. We awkwards

must go wandering, and tend in our lives
most happily to

doorways set in hillsides upon which we made
human departures and human trade.

Speech in a Chamber

In this book birds are taught their flying
by that which would make them fall
were they not to fly as had been taught.

The book is roughly bound, and left
open on a couch. The page is illustrated
and, lifted to the light displays

a moralizing scene: two children have tied
a third to the wheel of an enormous carriage.
A group of elderly women look on with pride.

It is a scent of such astonishing strength,
why, Leopold, there are flowers hidden
throughout the room. There must be for I

cannot sleep without the noise of a bouquet,
and gently, gently, sir, you know
I sleep most gently in this small room.

Speech Confided

A sheaf of worthy papers, set in a wheel and made to spin
may be enough to give
shape to a hundred ill-set lives.

I declined the first, as it was not freely given.
I declined the second, as it was scarcely a ribbon

bound about a child's throat.
And that I do not care to lead.
The third was charity.
The fourth came with my fame.
Yet sadly I relate, I could not deny the fifth.
For she spoke so clearly of things I have desired.

And so she sits, even now in the rooms above
plotting when she weeps and weeping when she plots.

A thought came yesterday that pleased me, my young
    friend.
When I die I shall send her a note, inviting her to join me
where I've gone. I'm told the dead can leave notes,

on the backs of leaves, in the brims of hats, on the inside
of a lady's glove.

Oh Leopold, the notes this shade will send . . .

Speech by a Window

For the sightless, shapeless hope is vision,
cast back by the long thrower like a discus,
heavy like a discus, ridged, impacted.
No vision is given once, nor given
only to one man, one woman, though legends
would have it so. Most dreams come
a hundred times in a given city before

waking the one who will raise it like some new
roof that men may live beneath.

Picture it, dawn in this far place.
The populace beginning to rise. Heads poking
out windows. Doors opening. Horses
standing in their stalls, their heavy breath
expectant. In the street, women with baskets
pass by house after house. In one
I myself wake. To me it seems
that what was true in the night
is far truer at daybreak. And bearing
this ribbon, I go out with a heavy coat,
with burned eyes, trembling hands.

There is a meeting on the riverbed
conducted with the utmost grace.
—these circumstances like a holstered gun,
that surprises by turn gunman and fool.
Through such waters others go
in boots sewn for the purpose.

Such boots, have I longed for anything more?
I will wear them in the open air
while elsewhere I am buried. And you
will read from Tuolti, who says,

The greatest hunter can hunt his prey and nothing else.
Others decide later
what was his prey, what was not.

One does not feel throughout one's life that one is always the particular age that one is. Rather, there are various stations in which one settles one's identity. As that station becomes unfit, or as one becomes unfit for that station, a new station must be reached. I, for instance, believed myself in many ways to be a child up until two or three weeks ago. Now I feel that I have lost something. But what I have lost is not childhood. It is not the freedom of childhood; that, I preserve. No—instead I have lost the time in which I was free to imagine myself a child. But what of it? I can still wrap a blanket around my shoulders and hide under rocks and bushes. I can still run through the house as fast as I can, run up and down the stairs as fast as I can. Why is it that we all have a tender spot in our hearts for bank robbers? Is it not because banks should be burned, because money itself is a vile creation? The disrespect of property is a religious propensity, and should be regarded as such.

2

PERHAPS

it is best to think of myself as an animal, as a bird with a coat of feathers crouched in the space beneath a bush. A place to live, a way to eat; nothing more. My own entertainments I can provide, and too my own teachings.

Without knowing, therefore, what I am after, I head once more into the hills. Up a path, up a road, along a wall. I pride myself on the variety of my foolish physical expression. One moment I am sulking, the next capering and taunting storm clouds. I believe that, were it possible, you might one day meet with me and be thus then affrighted by my terrible aspect. That is to say—at this moment, I am a robber set foot in the public sphere. Do you like my pistol? my dagger? Whatever you answer, you must admit, I carry them boldly. Boldly, yes boldly, I go into town any time I please. Not for me to fear the wag of tongues. *Oh, sir, do you recognize me from two nights' past when I erupted from the road to steal your carriage?* Well, then, a duel. Let us to it. So you see I am not afraid of CIRCUMSTANCE, and court it with my every gesture. OF COURSE there are those times, those times when tired and empty of myself, I walk past some brightly lit cottage where a supper of some sort happily is being conducted. It's then that the long years of rascalry sit heavily on my shoulders. OF COURSE it is of no account, for should I choose, there's many a winsome maid who'd have me in her house and household, setting up and settling up the days and hours. Yes, the peculiar quality of my life is that I allow myself to think that nothing yet has been excluded. Everything is still possible, and in the meantime I take to the hills and prey upon lone carriages and go with my hands gloved in the finest cloth.

second parts of this complicated Amazonian hospital in the faltering construction of a dream.

7

Without knowing the names of the men who came this way once, gathered up in this same foolishness which I call strength, I rejoice nonetheless in their companionship in their invisible sovereignty—for surely each has been and is suzerain of some single portion of this clever map? Today I resolved to count things in days to take the uselessness of the week and the day of the week and their names and make it still more useless by lettering any letters seventeenth Sunday of the year, fifth Tuesday, thirty-second Friday. Yes, yes, you have perhaps received already one of my frantic letters dated thus on the back: Thirty-fourth Thursday of my twenty-seventh year. I wonder if you took heart at this small uselessness. I wonder if you smiled and braved your way through some season of filth and disease using small kindnesses that I bestowed on you as breviaries or crutches, as pigeons to be mocked and chased. Chase and they shall lead you to the cote where I sit with a good warm bottle of spirits and a fist of chocolate. We shall go on sitting in secret and we shall, I promise you, let no one know what of we speak. And how the portioned day advances never by portion. I refuse its fingertips when they come slipping through my pockets and setting my coat upon my shoulders. Merely because another wants me to go out? Is that reason enough? It is clear to me that the greater part of happiness is to be found in spending as much time as possible roused and gone out from the place in which one sleeps. Yet how to do this simple thing? Even now I write "roused and gone out " yet I'm within my chamber—is it unseemly not to take one's own advice? But I do, I do. I am a taker of my own advice such as there has never been in this world, and there are many who think me difficult because of it. But there are others—and how sweet their faces are, come calling in my recollection—who see my gladness in the midst of my contrary nature and it is my gladness they go greeting. It is my gladness therefore that goes to greet them that goes walking with them, impromptu, incandescent, ensconced like a glittering mote in the eye of a sometimes pharaoh who calls upon cats and only cats to navigate this much folded kingdom of days.

8

Going out now and then with a heavy wig upon his shoulders Marzipan was soon overwhelmed by the trading of insults that any outward endeavor soon become in these forthright, claptrap, and cancerous times. Have I shown you the masks I made in these days? the lovely daily masks made for business purposes? A mask for the bakers, a mask for the bank, a mask for gardening, for correspondence. I took myself here and there like a leaf in a dry season, framing my replies with all of my heart. If I knew the interlocuter, if I praised the arbiter with a moment's pause in my rambling interrogations, then who can speak slightingly of my influence? Some are born in latter times with great capability for grasping certain facts, certain ideas, but not others, and so, when they go wandering in their father's garden that is the past they receive only half the take of their ears. And I , little gray flower at the pond's edge, make no case for myself on the long corridors of history. My time was wasted in speaking with frogs in treating with minor devils of time and armature. I who lapped happily at my own edges, gracing the lips of an October machination, was soon party to the dream sendings of just such an incorporeal statesman of the old sort, bearded, you understand, decorated in blood (all duelists of note, retaining nothing if not their word as bond). They sowed amongst themselves no good season giving onto season and now the walls shudder before the might of an evening no parlor or parlor game can dispel. Go out Millicent, to the porch and see what he wants, go at once.

9

M. Lion Tamer, a puppeteer of no real note, begins each performance with the saying of a Roman proverb. How much I like him for that. Yes, that and the press of

the crowd as Christmas nears. Lights have been hung
throughout the city center and happiness like coins de-
feats for a moment the ground of sorrow.

10

In a golden room I will resolve on all my futures, plac-
ing days like ranked and filed soldiers into passes,
bridgeheads and river crossings that must at all costs
be held.

11

Not without fault then the arrival of the vain, the timo-
rous, the sounding of their names one by one on the roof-
tops where we wait with hooks and nets for their leader
who comes in the guise of concealed laughter. In my coat,
the pistol that's to be used. My hand was trembling when
I took it. I am young and not used to these things.

12

My love I want only to go to the sunlit chamber above
tables and chairs I would push aside spreading space I
would lay a sheet upon the ground a sheet of soft cot-
ton and I would say is it soft enough my love? and you
would stretch and lie upon it and rise, saying, "it is not
soft enough," and I would lay another sheet upon the
first, saying, my love is it soft enough? and you would
stretch and lie upon it and rise saying only, my love it is

not soft enough. and so for the laying of nineteen sheets, of softest cotton, and the sun.

13

Not through any change of color do they blend with their environment but rather through a native instinct. First he matches the footsteps of a fellow and seems to go with him, seems in company. Next he is beside a woman—he seems her husband. Her child immediately appears as his daughter. So convincing the part, so regal. But does she take his hand? We cannot say for sadly we have lost them in the press on this hot day in one or another delinquent later month.

14

It was a sort of typewriter, but for writing on thin stone tablets. They watched as the man expertly tapped away here and there on the keys. In a moment, something was prepared! He pushed it into a slot in the wall. A door opened on the far side of the room.

—Some sort of death certificate, said Macalister. But for whom?

—Oh, don't say that, said Lorna. It can't be.

They shrunk together against the hard wall of the cell.

Could it be that the Aztec god was an enormous stone adding machine?

Macalister thought back. If only he'd kept a hold of his "thunder-stick." Then they wouldn't be in this mess. He glared impotently at the guard, who was busy drawing a pictograph of Lorna in her modern-style underwear.

15

A LIE HAD BEEN SPREAD

A lie had been spread throughout the court, that he who would kill the King would have the Queen's gratitude and would rule beside her. When a man rose up and killed the King, he was captured by the guards and brought before the Queen, who gave him but one prerogative, that he would forever set the manner of punishment that should befall regicides, and that he himself would begin this new tradition. To which the man, sensible of the great honor being done him, replied with a complicated and elaborate manner of death, one that would require an enormous preparation of years, and the expenditure of great wealth. And the Queen set the preparations in motion, and put the resources of her kingdom to this task, and laboured beside the man for fifteen years, until she was no longer a great beauty, and he seemed to her to be no longer the man who had killed her husband, but another man, of newer and more valuable vintage. Yet to his death the man went, in a ceremony so grand that the kingdom was beggared. The execution itself took an entire year, during which no one in the land was allowed to labor. General fasting was required, with the taking of only water allowed, and only that once a day. When the man died in the specified manner, of grief at the loss of a kingdom of lives, the land was barren and corpse-ridden, and the next traveler to come that way was puzzled at the immense arena which stood in the midst of an empty city, with the body of the regicide set atop a pillar at its very center.

16

Why do I always return to the forest path again and again? The forest path, the forest path with all its attendant resources—the hiding of animals, of people, the dangers, the dimness at midday while near in a clearing the shuddering of full day and dens and burrows beautiful beneath the ground how long days seem when they reach and reach again to their full length and stretch themselves so kindly along the forest path! Shall we go then now and see? Would that I was not so far from the forest. Would that even now I might see with these old eyes the forest path.

You laugh at my odd bearing, my pauses in speech. You smile at my uncouth abode. Yes it is true, I live in what might be called a meager hut in a filthy dell, set in a wood between hither and yon. Yes it is true, I wriggle in my disguise and seek with each breath to escape. I was, you know, once a fox. Someone tricked me into this human shape and here I will remain until I die. A little girl told me once words of comfort:

you'll be a fox again when you've gone to your grave.

It cost her nothing to say it, but for me it was a matter of great pain.

17

At the hurdy-gurdy factory, the Master-Builder was selecting melodies. His office was like the inside of a massive harp. Everything was possible with him. One was afraid even to move.

—Sir, I yelped.

I was waving some letter, some nonsensical letter. I don't even know where it came from, but it was very dirty, and distasteful even to hold.

—Sir, I yelped. Sir!

But that day was soon finished, and the one after it, and now things have gone so far I can't even say whether this was my memory or my grandfather's, the violent man whose grave I share.

And with waking now upon a particular morning and before you, worlds and doors locked once, left open, particular and inconceivable. Shall we go out this way and down the avenue? shall we enter by the garden gate and slip up the unlocked stair to the room beneath the roof? the unkempt room that once was let to German boarders, young men and such, engaged always in the study of some or another mathematics?

18

Licorice . . . it was considered a poison by the Romans, and acted in fact, quite well in this regard, save that, as it possesses none of the qualities of a true poison, its victims would have to be informed of their fate. This led to scenes that were often parodied by persons blessed by history with a better understanding. Yet think of this, and think clearly for once—the taste of licorice . . . does it not recall to you something? Its taste is misplaced. Somewhere, an error was made and never rectified. The question nonetheless remains, who first discovered its safe use in confections? Thousands of people must have died before some tribune or proconsul proclaimed it safe. And then, how confusing a thing it must have been the survivors. How sad the fate of those reached last by the news, some proud couple living in a manse on the far frontier, self reliant, comforted by their own strength. The messenger finds only their bodies. I don't believe anyone knows any more about this.

It has been long believed that wind is due to pressure differences in the air. However, the recently published research of Ch. Stevens of Greenwich has called this theory into question. Through painstaking observation he has noticed that while pressure differences seem to account for wind, they only *approximate* how wind might be, leaving us with two possible conclusions—the first that it is not pressure at all that determines wind, but something else entirely, and the second, that some common thing determines and influences both wind and pressure differences, and that the discrepancy between the two is caused by the influence of some third factor. The question then, what is the third factor, has been the work of Stevens' life. He discovered the discrepancy as a child poring over charts, but told no one for sixty-five years as he set about cementing his theory of the THIRD FACTOR.

The THIRD FACTOR is, Stevens believes, observation by man or animal. His thesis in particular explains the sudden escalation of tornadoes and tsunamis which hitherto have been scientifically unexplainable. Furthermore, Stevens has posited an enormous sea eye lying at or near the center of the fabled Bermuda triangle.

19

said the soldier to the grackle king:

I am glad of this theatre you so joyously provide, for I

travel by foot and by picturing myself still farther down these roman roads.

20

I drew you aside once, do you remember it? We were young—you four, I three, we had been put for safe-keeping in the charge of a farmyard. Everyone was cruel and we couldn't see why. We went apart to a shallow ditch in the back of a goose pen and sat in the shade of wet ground. I don't remember what was said but there was much. We talked all day and into the night, and the searchers discovered us by the moon's broken spokes. I often think of that conversation, often feel my life has been the length of those words, those scratched diagrams and shapes in mud. Did we leave the wiser? What did I tell you, so important, a thing I now don't know save in mourning and loss?

21

The apologies rendered me by the provincial mayor were, I must say, quite insufficient. I coughed merely and looked into my sleeve while his aide de campe blanched at the insult done. But what matter is it to me? If I choose I may change into a cloud or a stone and sleep for a century until all living are now dead. I have done so before and there is no trouble involved. Only an undoing of buttons, an unhooking of hooks, a light wheeling of countenance here and then about.

22

The red cloth that you named Garment Beamer and how you wrapped all your things in it, so many and joyful, and went with me gladly as I sang a song of warders and the wide advance. We climbed a well and were lost to what we knew. Then, afterwards, the day of whistled faces and crowns, the lunches prepared in our honor by a man we had seen once in a shop and thought vaguely respectable.

23

In a dream, I come upon a sort of paramilitary canteen. An attack is being readied. People of all sorts, dressed in civilian garb are standing about, remonstrating with each other, preparing themselves. There are great quantities of weapons, presided over by older men, precise fellows of a Swiss type. There was a place to be shoed, a place to be jacketed, belted, etc. Shall I say that the guns were quite odd? Most were of a sort, as was explained to me—oh, I should say first, just then everyone left. It had begun. I was standing there, and the great mass of people left the place of armament and went off into the town. The sound of gunfire came from almost every direction. Still, in the armory I felt quite safe. I talked with one of the men who explained that these weapons they were distributing were of a peculiar sort fit for revolution. They were three shot pistols, firing shotgun shells. They could not be reloaded. Once the pistol was done, perhaps recourse to a knife? I did not ask him this. The main thing is, the pistol could also be used as a grenade, in which case all three shells would explode simultaneously. — *Very effective,* he explained. No one will have predicted this.

As a kindness he provided me with an old Remington break-barrel shotgun with which to make my way East. It was predicted the countryside would rise. But if they did not?

24

I fought with 3 older children in my father's garden. What right had they to be there? They are painted, garish like a festival and I am wearing the plainest of clothes. They are older all and speak with authority of matters out in a world to which I have never gone.

And yet, it is my father's garden. I approach them even now and the quarrel begins anew.

25

I came, when all the rest had gone, with many fine things to say and do. We went as tinkers through the farthest settlements in the fifth of your five lives. So often you would say to me if only our lives had been laid head-to-head and foot-to-foot—instead this brief exchange of shipwright and wind having less to do with what is known than with what we would know and tell.

26

The flea perched on the chair's back reports with utmost fury: *There are no studies so foolish as those taken up with another's leave.*

27

Of not less than three I speak now coming in rain in dubious transport through borders of clay and roadways of stone. The mast is off course and next shall cause— treason, which is the poor man's chance, dubbed fortune in an era of coalbins and apple trees.

28

A project:

1. Find a man out for a walk with his two children, both of a portable and inconsiderable age. Though old enough for memory's sake. Say five or half past four.

2. Come upon this man in prepared union with a friend (you and a friend or confederate). Spring upon him

in a park, seizing both children when they are equidistant from the man. This is crucial: we will discuss why later.

3. Proceed to kidnap the children, running away at a hasty, but not overwhelming pace. You therefore force the man to choose from between his children which is to be saved. When he takes up chase the one pursued will lead him upon a merry run for a short stint providing time for the other to escape. When that aim has been accomplished (and presumably then the father will be close) the child will be set down neatly and escape will be easily effected for the father will then stop to take care of his stolen child. And meanwhile, the other captor is well away and safe, having succeeded in the theft.

NOW

4. The stolen child in step 4 will be kept away for a period not longer than one calendar day. Following that period of separation, he will be returned safe and sound to the bosom of his family.

5. It is crucial to understand here that while the child is held in illegal custody it will be supported in high style, given various treats and placated in countless inventive and surprising ways. Then the child will be taught about the event that has transpired. It will be made most carefully to understand that in an even contest, its

father's affections were led to choose its brother rather than itself. How sad the child will be then. Perhaps it will be shown footage of the crucial incident such that it can see for itself how its father abandoned it to a cruel and uncertain fate. Then, as we say, the child is returned secure in the knowledge that its father chose not to save it.

6. The plan now proceeds to stage six. Immovable bronze statues depicting each boy, the father and the kidnappers will be placed in the park in correct relative position complete with dedication and name-plates. At the induction ceremony the family will be invited and the entire matter explained to the press.

7. However uncomfortable things are in the happy home, they will be made still more, for a sum will be laid on the stolen unchosen (by his father) boy and provided annually and overlooked such that he is capable of a standard of life of which his brother and family could never hope to attain.

THEN the chosen child will wish himself Unchosen and all will be quite grand for of a Sunday in the park as they grow older and age into death they will now and again come upon these statues and remember deeply and indefatigably their father's true choice.

Meanwhile in the forest the door to the very largest tree had been left open and all manner of creatures whether desired or not could come and go through all and any rooms of the great and complicated house that he had made both at once in passing in a childhood conversation and later with his own two hands from a place of hiding. Who then to come once and for all and set matters straight?

30

I was nevertheless famous in many circles, my name known, for instance, to those who dwelt alone, to those who drew water in silence at midnight from the well at the world's heart.

31

A character who enters the scene, always by balloon.

32

An Egyptian painter whose lettering and figure work was so precise it far surpasses the precision and accuracy possible today through the use of machines.

33

I should like very much to have a shop in the downstairs section of some boarding house or general store that I own. The employee would sit behind a desk dressed well, and would make boldfaced lies to whoever comes in. These lies would in some sense be regimented, for instance, no promises of any kind would be made.

A man came to Inilvick out of a great storm repeating over and over the seventeen characters and fourteen formulations that make up the long lost language of the countryside. For once in Inilvick man had the faculty of speaking with animals and such as he liked. For that reason, though the old arts are long lost, all the best animal trainers of the fourteenth century were born in Inilvick.

Some began the meeting with loud angry or dissatisfied talk while others shrank together at first out of fear but sometimes verging into inappropriate groping. I admonished a handsome woman who sat beside me in a dress having no fewer than 93 buttons: WHY MUST YOU WEAR SO MANY BUTTONS? to which she opened wide her pretty mouth to show 3 rows of sharpened teeth.

Cleverly we accord no respect to wily makers of intricate toys or to the writers of wire-thin stories that confound even the kind attentions of dressmakers crouched resolutely in a sultan's hourglass with precise, indeed all-comprehending instructions.

OH the long winters! Yes, we in Lundil do survive from year to year, or so we are told, but the tactics we must employ, though perhaps obvious, are lamentable and leave us powerless to know how things were in the previous year, or even who we were. What of my associations? What of my medals, my friendships? What of our great tradition of letter-writing, second only to the town of V. far down the river? Well, each year we of the town congregate and are assigned notes as in some staged production. It is then, in the aftermath of four months' hibernation, in which dreams have emptied our minds of all true import, that we can slip with impossible ease, into our new roles, like the scissored rain clouds of some failed attempt to render the ever-present sky.

38

Goodbye, again, and all of them going off down to the shore, and out to sea. Well, we shan't see each other again I say, not in this life, and then I too am off into the waters, swimming at my resolute, far-grasping pace. We shall not see each other again, I say, but how long life is, and how foolish all predictions. Throw me ashore on some desert coast sweep me up on some eastern river: All that I plan is replaced with that which I dread in a manner so very predictable I find I often see the world makers' hand. Yet what then? Knowing you are being tricked is no help if you can find no one to tell you why.

39

Though it is often said that Noah escaped the flood due to a warning from God, we find it much more likely that he happened anyway to be building a boat and happened anyway to be amassing a living record of the world, that he happened anyway to be at sail on that particular day when the skies opened. In short it was a mixture of diligence and chance that saved him from that which claimed all other lives. Yet he is not alone in this. For plague is as voluminous as water, as all-seeing, as dark-minded. I shall speak of those who have built arks with which to weather that deft and thriftless horror, the bubonic plague.

40

I leap down from the still-moving train and cry out to you—

after so long, I have arrived at last.

—Have you then, arrived at last, you say doubtfully, and this dream too is confined to a place of disrepute and forfeit.

41

No! No!

And with that the curtains break from the ceiling and fall, crushing the almost imperceptibly tiny figures below in immense and incarcerating folds.

42

And with the light of a sudden fields appear and houses, hills topped with green and gray outcroppings of stone.

43

Those there are walking alone with a stick in black night that come now at once with me to day. In the wood where the reddest bird draws on its beak and ascends to its body, there I will wait and consider what first I will say.

44

Pastimes are arranged so precisely in this collapsible season to prepare for the arrival at any moment of a still greater conception. This is to say the youngest and prettiest girls put on their best clothes but do not go out or even rise to answer the door.

45

Recording the moment of his death in the twelfth century, Abbot Corgris had himself dipped in ink and placed on a thirty-foot-square piece of drawn cloth. Has the record since been lost? I have not seen it in my travels to England's abbeys and convents, but of course, someone could be treasuring it, keeping it in a sacred place and looking glowingly upon it from time to time. It is said his sprawling death moved him first towards the top of the canvas and then away down and left.

46

A large animal attacked a child between four and five crowds that had been on the avenue. Neither the fourth nor the fifth was there. One had left, one was to come. The child was alone. Then, a rustling in the bushes. A large animal; yes, a large animal. Presumably it tore the child limb from limb or bit at it over and over while pinning it beneath a hideous forepaw. I really can't say exactly what happened having not been there and indeed never having heard of the incident until now.

47

I dug a hole with an antique trench shovel that my great grandfather brought back from the wars. It fits in the hand so nicely, it makes you wish there were more reasons to use a trench shovel. And how it folds up so deliciously and fits so precisely into its tarpaulin carrying sack! I decided then and there I would hate Mrs. Eddling whose place is next over. So, I began by pelting her with stones. When she responded badly to this, the line was drawn. I dug a trench clear across the yard. Eventually I will dig another and another until I reach the house. Then I will push her into a hole and use my antique shovel to throw dirt in until there's too much for her to bear and then I will rest and after a while finish the job, but oh my it is nice to have this spade and I really don't mind at all inventing reasons to use it. Don't you feel the same way?

I saw a man with the wind in a bag go about in a finely tailored suit here and there showing off his finely trimmed hooves and saying, dear sir, dear madamoiselle, are you aware that the show is about to begin?

Method of Secret Committee

Six to nine men or women are to be gathered, masked, and cleansed of recognizable detail. There each puts forward some task he or she needs solved. Then unbeknownst to the others, each takes on one of the other's tasks and performs it secretly.

Opening the vent, I am engaged, yes, desperately engaged, in moving the air from the outside in. It is this way with me that when I become furious and reach a red wall in my thoughts, I do not speak or make any outer countenancing, but go straightaway to this place and open the vent. Thereafter shall follow, thereafter follows, events in which I can take no pride.

And shall we predict the passage of a certain young lady down the street? Yes, a certain young lady, a certain girl, wearing a rather stiff rubber suit. It is a punishment enacted by her father, a veterinarian. He is pleased to drive very thin pins into the back of her neck which swell at his command.

What if you were told of this behavior of his? What if you were witness to it in his house, brought there as a guest? Do you have within you the strength to stand up to him? He seems sometimes to be at least a hundred feet tall, with a face as deep as an avenue.

At the edge of these reflections, there is a little closet into which one can sometimes cram oneself. Then to sit there until everyone has gone, and the house is empty! I wonder, have the hallways of my youth extricated themselves from all our foolish pranks?

The knife strikes here and there, thin as a bird beak, and wanting as much to satisfy some undisclosed covenant of shape that stands as a rebuke to our present geometry.

Do I desire to have the dresses from the backs of all the loveliest workers in this cruel factory? Is it in the name of an inspection that this will be done? Then what smooth well-formed limbs, what lithe shoulders, what slender waists . . . are not the women of our collective beautiful? Indeed it is sometimes said that in the factory they are not forced to work at all but only to bathe and groom and shape themselves in long cool tiled rooms while discussing philosophy. Is it true? Is such a hideous rumor true? Well, I confess, our truest natures are to be found in lunacy, and it is over such a realm that I preside, even now. Out with the lamp!

56

How disappointing it is to find that so many of the doors one comes upon in the hills and between the streets, yes in the town where you were born, beside the towering hospital, lead nowhere and do not give onto that great and stretching second world for which you hope and hope.

57

Defeating the world's strongest man in a fight does not make you the world's strongest man, just as killing Jesse James does not make you Jesse James.

58

The King is the first: all must obey him, at least when in his presence. That is why the King keeps a court—in order to enlarge his presence.

59

I went out without my coat. The day was too cold, and I suffered there in the street, going about my business. Small women and men called to me with their paltry voices. A dog was attaching itself to a very beautiful girl where a green spread of grass met the street. She was using both hands to keep her skirt down, and the weather was bad.

Won't you help me? she cried.

But I love another and she is gone into a far country from where I cannot retrieve her.

60

Pheasants and scatterguns, alphabets, charms, phrases, curses, naysayers, nickel machines, mistaken identities. It was all too much for little Alphonse, who cluttered his brain with anything anyone happened to say to him. He went about in a little blue suit rather worn at the knees and a little paper satchel stitched with his initials. — Hello, he would often say, whether anyone was there or not. — Hello, I am with the name Alphonse and I am so lucky I can't tell you. Would you believe more than one woman fell for this trick and got right into bed with him? Well, yes, it is true. They properly waited no more than five or ten minutes upon making his acquaintance to take him across the doorstep, etc. But did this please our Alphonse? We shall say rather that he delighted in meat pastries and thought foremost of this gluttony above and beyond all others. He was, it is said, a fixture at the shop of Baker Morton, who despised him and beat him relentlessly whenever the poor boy came into reach.

61

Has not the geometry of comparison, the superimposition of another land on this present land, become a bit wearisome to you who travel in our good company? One cannot go on using it in place of the eyes.

pieter emily

2006

Do Not
Take the
Low Road

The world is old, and wherever there is room for a body to sleep, there something has died.

— Pieter Emily, said they one to another in the furrows and fields.

— Pieter Emily, whispered they the children beneath the wooden boards of the raised village.

— Pieter Emily, said Elsbeth Grinner, beneath her breath.

And she left her loom and went out into the street.

It was a clear day and dry. Marla Kranth was standing speaking to the mayor's wife. Both wore long dresses and heavy shawls made from the cloth that was the village's trade.

— Marla, said Elsbeth, is it true?

— True and more, said Marla. He's breathing the same air as you or me.

The mayor's wife interrupted. Her face was narrow like a shrew, and it was said by some that she bit the mayor in his sleep to weaken his brain.

— Jasper spoke to him, face to face. Pieter Emily. Out on the low road, and Jasper looking for a sheep that had strayed. Pieter was there, behind a tree, just watching him.

— Pieter? On the low road?

Both women nodded in a dark, disapproving way.

—What did he say? asked Elsbeth.

—Pieter reminded him of the green book. He said it was late in the year for anyone to be out on the low road.

Marla whistled a long whistle.

—But what did he look like?

—Like a boy in a wooden-coat, said Marla. Just like he always looked. Jasper said he hasn't aged a day.

A week passed and a week. On the fourteenth day, Elsbeth closed up her shop early and sent the other weavers home. She was, it was generally agreed, the best of Forsk's weavers, and that meant she was one of the best in the world. For there is nothing like Forsk-cloth, and there never has been.

She was born with a feel for the thread. The day she touched a loom she knew it was a beast akin to her and that if only she would speak it would give her whatever she desired. So slowly and quickly, slowly and quickly she learned to speak to the loom, and when she was fourteen, she was given a shop, and given the charge of many weavers below her, and people who came to the town would sit on chairs in the corner of the room and watch her as she worked.

Since then, her skill had only grown. She could do in an hour the work of days, and in days, work that no one could do in any quantity of time. At the age of forty-three, she was thin like a reed, with a wicker strength. She wore only the simplest clothing, made from her own cloth and sewed in the closeness of her rooms.

She lived with her sister and her sister's husband, in a tall house set away at the edge of the raised town. It was not an outbuilding, as the farmhouses in the fields beyond. But it was thought less of, for once it had been a freestanding structure, and only during her childhood had the village grown to reach it with its tight wooden streets and walks.

She and her sister had been the same at birth. They had had the same dream every night of their common childhood, and would recount it anew each morning. But when Elsbeth was taken away to the loom, Catha took up the needle and thread. As a seamstress Catha had no match in Forsk. Her husband, Jaim was a trader, one of those who took the cloth through the mountains for sale. He was a large man, and of a wonderful quality. Catha loved him as a wife, and Elsbeth as a sister. For Jaim was sullen and ill-mannered in all save his speech with them. We should all be lucky to have such a one for a friend, and they knew his worth.

To that house, then, Elsbeth went, out her shop door and along the street. She passed shops where the people were crouched in rows before looms, or others where men and women were set to carding or spinning. The wood of the town was like a box, she often thought, with all that was needed laid out within it. Well, that and the fields beyond.

— Pieter Emily, she said beneath her breath.

They were the same age, she and Pieter, the same age to the day. His father had been a hunter, his mother, a weaver in the town. Their houses had stood side by side, looking in on each other, listening to each other's secrets in the long winters, the brief mists of summer.

It had been Pieter who'd shown her the way up trees. She in turn had taught him to lie. For Elsbeth Grinner was an expert liar and always had been. She had, in fact, never been caught in a lie. Not once. She was most certainly the soul of truth.

In fact, she had not lied in many years. There was no reason to. Her life was all seriousness, all cloth and candles, all evening.

As she went her way, a man came out from beneath the eaves of the grocery.

—Elsbeth, he said, have you seen this?

A handbill had been printed, and he gave it her to look at.

The MATTER of PIETER EMILY

+ +

Village Meeting

+ +

Third Bell from Dusk

Elsbeth nodded to the man.

— Harfor Locke, thank you. I shall see you there.

He retired again below the roof, leaving her with the handbill, as the other shops too closed and the street began to fill. Yet no one jostled her as they passed. Many looked to her and looked away, and those who met her eyes nodded respectfully. What the town did was what she did best, and strange as she was, she was admired by all.

An hour and she stood again with the handbill in the doorway. Her sister's shadow could be seen in the kitchens beyond, moving here and there.

Since Pieter Emily had been seen, a rash of trouble had begun. The farmers on farms closest to the low road had found animals dead, their throats cut. A house had even burned. Jerome Liddel vanished one day from his fields, and his wife was in tears in the streets asking for justice. Old Caleb More swore he saw a fox carrying a child in its mouth, but no child was missing.

Was it strange to think of a red fox in all that grayness, running with a white goose in its mouth? Many dreamed it, and wept upon waking, so lovely was the drawing in and out of breath in the goose's heaving chest.

— The green book, said they one to another.

Elsbeth passed by the kitchens but did not look in. Her sister looked up and saw her, but said nothing. She knew the degree, the direction of her thought. For once many had thought Pieter would ask Elsbeth's hand. But he had not, and then he had fallen out with Algren Johns and Leonard Falk, and had fought them together, with Saul Cross and Imren Jacoby, Locke Arsten and Jaim himself as witnesses, and Pieter had shot them both through the chest with a pistol. Yet Falk had been just as quick. Wounded by Falk's pistol ball, Pieter had staggered off into the woods. That had been twenty-five years ago. There hadn't even been a search for him. His mother had gone through the town again and again, begging for help. But something about Pieter had been dark, and no one would help. Catha's father had forbade them to go, and they had not. Then there was the matter of Algren Johns', of Leonard Falk's funeral. Time had simply passed, and drawn a quiet over the whole business.

If Elsbeth was as serious as earth on earth, then this last week had seen her grow grimmer still. Catha worried and worried, and by the fence with Jaim at first light, she'd asked him what they ought to do.

His face hadn't changed. He'd said nothing at first, and then,

—Something's likely to be done. Things can't go on like this.

And now there was the meeting. Anders Lew had knocked on the window at half three to announce it. What would be said? She shuddered in spite of herself and hurried on with the preparations for supper.

One bell. Two bells. Three bells in the dusk, and the people came through the streets.

Elsbeth walked with her sister. Jaim trailed behind, speaking to the smith, Canter Maynard.

So many steps in the thin darkness of the town. Lamps were at every corner, and the wood gave a comfort, a drumming as of life.

As she walked, Elsbeth thought of the pattern she'd begun that morning. She could see all the threads in her head, could watch them shaking and forming together, twining and joining. She wanted then to go to the shop and sit down at her loom, but her sister's hand on her shoulder recalled her.

—Are you all right?

—Just thinking.

And then they were at the meeting house. And then they were taking seats near the back. Almost the whole town was there, some three hundred. Only half the farmers, of course. The flocks and fields had, after all, to be watched, most of all now.

Looking around, Elsbeth saw fear in the shapes of backs and necks, the imposition of heads on necks, the taking up of gowns and blankets, hands, white and gaunt, pressed against the benches.

How could she, of all people, find her way through this maze of confused words and thought?

The Mayor stood to speak.

He called for order, and after a while, the rumbling ceased.

—I stand here before you as an act of free election.

It was the invocation called for at the beginning of every meeting.

—A matter has risen that needs a consensus. The murderer Pieter Emily has been discovered living not fifteen miles from this spot where I stand.

A great noise then rose up in the hall. Rumor, certainly, had had its way with the town. Everyone had heard Jaspar Mign's tale, whether from he or another. But this was the first general confirmation of its truth.

—Order, order, shouted the Mayor.

He slammed a staff down on the raised platform and the crowd grew quiet.

—The facts of the matter, said the Mayor. Pieter Emily vanished almost 26 years ago, leaving two of the town dead. It matters not at all that it was a duel, or that they were two and he one. The rules forbade such duels then, just as they do now.

A man spoke up in the third row.

—My daughter saw a man inside our house not two days ago. From what we can tell, it was Pieter Emily!

A din rose up at this, with nearly every member of the town declaring themselves aggrieved in one way or another.

Then Jaspar Mign stood up, and all fell silent.

—He said the green book, said Jaspar. He said the green book, and now this is on us.

The meeting fell into chaos and nothing could be done for some time, with some swearing that Pieter was to blame for all the present ills, and others swearing that he was not. Someone began to draw up a vote on the matter, and the white and black painted sticks were brought out in the long, iron box, but the measure failed, and no vote was taken. Finally, the candles burned down and the meeting was closed, to be resumed on the next day, and everyone was sent home.

Elsbeth prepared herself for sleep. She laid her dress across a chair back, and stood by the window looking out across the hills. The night was clear and bright, and her sharp eyes could see far.

The village was in a hollow. It was like a great, wooden apparatus, laid out flat upon the ground. Hills and fields lay all around, and mountains as well. Mountains took up three horizons, and farther, the fourth. It was a long vale, and the road that ran down from Firsk to the far mountains was the low road. No one traveled it, or spoke of it. The town looked East, through the mountains. East was where trade was. East was the world. To the West, who knew? People had gone there once. But the green book had been written during a time of trouble in the village, and by following its rules, the village had grown and prospered. Look east, urged the green book. Do not take the low road.

Elsbeth shivered in the sudden cold and ran her hands over the thin bones of her ribs, the flatness of her stomach, her narrow legs. She ate rarely, her sister told her, but Elsbeth thought rather that she was like the threads of the loom, that she had grown only more like them with time, and that it was this oneness that allowed her her single pleasure.

For to see the shuttle in her hands was like nothing else, like air through air, like needles through needles.

The first sleep came and went. Elsbeth rose and set to her ledgers. She could do nothing with them, though, and in the midst of turning a page, she was pierced by the sudden remembrance of a dream.

A child was blowing a whistle louder and louder, and as the whistle grew in sound, the wind came through the teeth of the mountains and the town began to break.

Elsbeth was in the meetinghouse again, and the meeting continued. But all the townspeople were dressed as animals. They wore the clothes of men, but each had the head of some sheep, some cow, some dove or swan or rat. A mouse with a stick stood on the platform. A frog with a drawn dagger raised it up in a webbed hand. She felt at her own face, but there was nothing there to feel, and she was again in the snow at the day's edge, where light was just breaking through a closing door.

I must speak to him, she thought.

—I must warn him, she said.

And the rustling of night that was listening at the window went away like salt over a shoulder.

Elsbeth dressed. She stood at the very center of the room. The tenth bell rang. She sat heavily on the floor. She stood again.

There are children among us, and in us, she thought. We

are guided by what we have been just as much as what we are. If I was at his side so often in the past, should I not now go to see what has become of the present time?

And in a room below, Catha sat with Jaim talking, and Jaim said it had been declared by many that Pieter would be brought to trial.

Yet he disapproved.

—It was no fault of his, said Jaim slowly. Falk had it in for him from the first, and goaded him and goaded him.

Falk, the present mayor's brother. The present mayor's name was Galvin Falk and he hated no one so much as Pieter Emily.

Did we say there was no search on that day twenty-five years ago? Say then there was rather a hunt. Galvin Falk led some dozen men through the woods again and again, scouring the underbrush for some trail of blood or scent. Dogs were called, nets laid across saddles. Down they went, all down to the low road, where they stopped, gathering their horses' necks close.

—If he's gone further, then he's damned.

And they rode back.

Firsk was not known to many, for the towns that had its trade were jealous of this trade, and would not share it. The truth is, the prices they paid Firsk's traders were nothing to the prices their traders received from farther traders. This was the same as one went from town to town, farther and farther, with each place valuing the cloth, yet knowing still less about it.

Each spring, the traders of Firsk would reach the towns just beyond the mountain passes. They would come with many mules, laden down. They would set up a broad bazaar and sit cross-legged, smoking long pipes and muttering strange rhymes.

Much ill was said of these men. Jaim, for instance, knew they were disliked by those in the world. But they were honored too, for was it not their trade that meant the most?

Yet now the world had been dispelled by the drought.

She dressed and wrapped a coat around her and, taking up a stick, went out into the night. First along the planked street, and then off into its ending, and down a stair to the fields beyond. The road was there, a slight ways off. There was hardly a moon, and the darkness was thick, but growing thinner. She stumbled to the road and set out in truth.

The mountains rose, etched as a matter of edges on the dim sky. The trees appeared in strength as she reached the edges of the farmland, the grazing meadows, and came in truth to where the town ended.

On she walked, stumbling sometimes in the muddling dark, off through the trees where the road lay. I am on the low road, she told herself, and a panic rose that fell away only when she recalled herself to what it was she had to do.

I must tell him.

And a light came then behind her eyes as she saw once again the landscape of days gone. They were digging a tunnel, she and Pieter, beginning in the hidden center of a bush, and passing away down into the cellar of Pieter's father's house.

Pieter was standing by the bush and calling to her. She held a spade in her hand.

— Elsbeth, he said. Come now, there's little time.

Elsbeth shook her head. The sun was rising. Had she been asleep? The sun was rising, setting the dark aside in the eastern reaches of the sky. She thought she saw movement in the trees. Was it a man? First behind one tree, then out from behind a farther tree. She was sure of it.

Fifteen miles. Fifteen miles she'd walked and now the sun was rising. She was out beyond where anyone had business going, out beyond where anyone had gone. The road rose. She looked over her shoulder, but could see no more motion in the woods. Just the rattling of birds, the stirring of insects.

The road rose and fell away down down down a long slope. The trees seemed to overtake the road on both sides, and the wood grew thicker and thicker as her eye passed farther into the distance. Yet there the road was again, and again, winking at turns.

And there, away on the right, a hill, and on the hill, a house.

— Pieter Emily, she said. And she set off again.

The house was simply built but strong, thick wooden beams all around, and a thatched roof of the old sort. There were many narrow windows all around, and a door set in the ground that must lead to a cellar.

On the step at the front, a man was sitting.

—Elsbeth, he said. You've come.

How he could have passed so many years without changing, she couldn't say, but it was true. She knew him immediately and completely. His eyes were narrow and gray. His face was thin and young. His hair fell wild from his head. He wore a simple coat, simple trousers and boots. He was not tall, he'd never been tall. He looked young at first, but there was something old too, something old and far that rose in him when he came to his feet.

—Pieter, she said. They are going to come for you.

He shrugged and looked away west.

—Will you come in?

Then up the steps and through the open door.

Shall I describe the fineness of Pieter's little house? The walls were thick, with beds and cupboards, shelves and chairs, even a table all inset. The narrow windows drove the light like lace here and there patterned on each opposite wall, so that the house was strung through with a mist of sun.

Pieter lit the stove at the room's center, and set water to boil.

—Sit now, he said. For it is no short way you've come.

—There's been a meeting. They will come here, I don't know when. They know you're here now.

Her voice was full of concern.

—It is kind, he said, for you to worry, but let us speak of it no more.

And he set before her a basket of flat cornbread.

—We are old friends, he said, come together again. Let us speak of gladder things.

Elsbeth rose and crossed the room. Here and there were hung tools and devices. A long axe, a lantern, a drawknife, a pair of gloves that would cover the arm up to the shoulder.

And set upon a shelf, the green book.

She took it up. The cover was thick, the book was like a flat tablet, for it enclosed only three leafs within.

Pieter poured the water into a tea-pot, and brought out two thin porcelain cups.

—Where did you get all these things? You did not re-turn to the town.

—Where did I get all these things? asked Pieter, lifting a saucer. It has been a very long time I have lived here alone, with no use for porcelain.

His eyes looked out as if through the wall.

—I will tell you a story, he said. A dog passes along the street. It sees a child. The child turns and looks in through a window, seeing a woman. The woman cuts herself with the sharp arm of a scissor, and cursing the scissor, sees her husband on a ladder at the far window, sees him and watches as a wind rises suddenly, inexplicably, and casts him off the ladder down into the street where the first person to reach him finds him dead.

Elsbeth narrowed her eyes.

—What do you mean?

—I will tell you a story, he said. A bird circles in the air, and sees with its length of sight a child crossing a stream, hopping from stone to stone. Someone is calling to the child, calling it back, but it reaches the far side, a field of tall grass. In a moment the grass is turned and grows into the shapes of some procession, a vast procession of dancing shapes that overtake the child and carries it away deeper and deeper into the field, until the procession vanishes and the grass is as it was, grass, standing grass, and the child is gone.

—I have been so long here, he said. With no one to speak to.

Elsbeth poured the tea, and tasted the cornbread. She finished the first and took another. Pieter smiled.

—What is that? Elsbeth asked.

For set in one wall there was a tiny bed, three feet long and two feet wide. It was made up with a quilt and a pillow, and even a small doll of rope and feathers lay on one side.

—There was a little boy, said Pieter, and he was born in the town. I came one day, keeping to the sides of things so no one could see me. I felt that if I brought the boy away with me, I could raise him as well as anyone. This was ten years ago.

—Cameron's child? exclaimed Elsbeth. Mora Cameron's child?

—I took him, I crept in the house and took him and carried him away. He was just born then, and I raised him myself. I took him everywhere with me through the wood, and carried him on my back. I taught him the songs of the morning, the long tales of night. I raised him as well as anyone could, as well as anyone. And he slept here, in the wall opposite my bed, where I could look in the night and see that all was well.

—But where is he? asked Elsbeth.

Pieter stood and a shadow passed over his face.

—He grew sick, he grew sick one day, and there was nothing could be done. He was dead by nightfall. I buried him out on the hill, with a stone for a pillow, and a name scriven on the stone and set beneath the ground.

—There was grief too in the town, when the child disappeared, said Elsbeth.

Pieter looked up and an unpleasant smile grew on his face.

—I think less of grief in the town, he said. Shall I tell you another story? A man goes walking in the woods and he meets another man, who he vaguely knows. He is guarded in his manner, perhaps even frightened. He has a weapon of some kind in his coat. He longs to have it in his hand, but there is no time for that, the strange man would see him reaching in his coat, would wonder why. And so they stand there talking and talking. *I must get back to the farm,* says the man. *There is much work to be done.* But the strange man lifts his hand. *No,* he says. *No. No work now to be done, but you shall come walking with me.* And so the men go walking further and further into the wood, and the wood changes. It changes from being of this year to being of another year, of no year. *Do not leave me here,* says the one. *For I do not know the way back.* But already the other is gone.

Elsbeth drank from her cup and the tea was hot and filled her with the far scent of oaks and trees in the deep wood.

She felt at once glad and safe, and also as if standing on a thin rope high above a flat country.

What am I doing here? she asked herself.

—I am sorry, she said, that I was no help to you when you fled the town. No one knew where you went, or even if you lived.

—Too long, he said. Too long ago to speak of.

—But they are speaking of it now in the town, said Elsbeth. They will come and take you. Don't you understand? It's not safe.

Pieter reached out his hand and touched her face.

—You can't worry, not here.

And the worry fell away.

THEN MANY THINGS
BETWEEN THEM WERE SAID.

Yes, in the day then there was the sitting in the house, the drinking of tea. There was the telling of stories, Elsbeth telling of her life, Pieter telling of his. There was the rising up, the out-of-doors, a walking in the woods.

—I was weaving, said Elsbeth, one day, a bolt of cloth, and there was no red in the thread, none at all, yet again and again, a red shape grew on the loom, small, here and there.

—I dreamt once, said Elsbeth, of a sea at the bottom of which our country lies. Those who live above take boats upon the sea and wonder at its depth, a depth so inconceivable that they dare not attempt it. They have myths and stories about the sea floor, but they know nothing of it. And here we think ourselves upon the highest plane, yet we stand only between things. There are seas here beyond the plains, and lands in the depths of those seas, just as we may look up through the slanting light and see the passing of ships in the heights of the sky.

—Have you, asked Pieter, seen this passing of ships?

—I have not, said Elsbeth.

—I have killed men, you know. Other than the two for which I fled. I have made the woods my own, and when others come there, I have come upon them and taken them, as I choose. I take animals in the woods, and I use their flesh for my table, their skins for clothing. I use their teeth for tools, their bones to build fences. When I have killed, I make a pile of stones, a cairn, and I set in my memory who it was, what it was that died there and how. My mind is shaped like a map of these cairns. My geography is the laying out of a great flatness peopled with cairns. One a bird, one a farmer, one a girl, one a deer. There are hundred, hundreds in the woods, for I have gone far and with great weight in my hands.

—There have been, said Elsbeth, some lost from the village, and no one knowing why.

But she did not feel any fear.

—Are you not afraid of me? asked Pieter.

—I am not afraid, said Elsbeth, not of you.

—Whether there is a name put to a place or not, still a place has a name, said Elsbeth. What do you call this place, or if you call it nothing, what does it call itself?

—I began, said Pieter, by walking around it twice. I began by discovering a place for a hidden field, a kind situation for animals. I began with winter here, and then spring, then summer, then fall, then winter again. But I did not think to name it until my house had stood full ten years with no visitor.

Elsbeth smiled.

—That is a fine name, she said, House-Without-Visitors. But now there is a visitor.

—You are not a visitor, said Pieter. Nothing that's mine is made without acquaintance of you.

Then they stood by the stream at the foot of the hill, where the roots of Lochen trees ran like a bridge here and there over it, and Pieter had made a bed for fish catching with the hands.

There was silver moss there.

Beneath a tree some distance into the forest, she could see a pile of stones.

—Who was it, she asked, died there?

A hare, said Pieter, the father of hares, the son of hares, an old hare, far gone through life. I caught him with a string trap and killed him with a knife.

—If I were to go first into a house of stone, and then into a house of wood, and then into a house of straw, and then into a bare roof set upon poles, and then to lie upon the empty ground beneath the sky with a blanket, and then even to cast the blanket aside and lie in the cold on the open ground, would you not think that I was making a grave for myself? For I can tell you that I have descended into what I am by throwing away the false edges of what I have been told. As I passed from house to house, the stone walls stayed with me, the wood supports, the pounded clay ground, the blankets, yet I threw them away. Everything you dismiss that is of use stays in the language of your hands. But I have seen your weaving, and I know you know the language of hands.

Elsbeth smiled and opened her hands looking down over them. They were thin hands with long fingers.

She thought of the darting shuttle that was so fine to hold, and of her shop as it stood now, empty in the town. There would have been no one to unlock it in the morning. Her workers would have come and gone. Someone would have called at her house, and found her absent. Catha would be wondering, where might she have gone. And there would be no answer. In the town there was no other place to have gone, nowhere verging into infinity, no place where one could not be found. Would eyes turn

—How is it that you live? asked Elsbeth. By hunting?

—I keep animals, and a field. I hunt in the long days, and sometimes at night. What you must understand is that when a person lives alone and sees no one, time is not like it is for others. There is so much time, so much time in the day I can't tell you. I have lived whole seasons in a single afternoon. What can be done in a day can be years and years of work, and in thinking, the end can truly never come. I have sat staring in a pool of water for weeks, and risen, half dead, but thinking only longer on the thought I found in the depths. I have dreamt at night of lives unlived in which I lived, in which I was born and lived full fifty years, sixty years, seventy years before dying and waking back into this life. What wisdom comes from such experience? What light trails back through these thrown-open windows? I become more and more as the objects of my alone-ness grow into extensions of my living.

—And west? Have you gone west? asked Elsbeth.

—I have, said Pieter, and he would say no more.

—Stay here awhile, said Pieter, for I must fetch our supper.

But I am not staying, said Elsbeth. I must return to town.

—You *can* stay for supper, said Pieter. You must.

And Elsbeth nodded in spite of herself.

When he was gone, she looked furiously around herself. Why had she agreed? She would leave a note, saying she had gone, saying she had had to go.

But there was no paper to be found save in books. And Elsbeth would not write in a book.

She walked about the house. There was another room, she noticed, at the house's back. She tried the door, but it was locked. She pushed against it, but it wouldn't give.

I wonder, she thought, what could be in this room? For the house as it was was stocked with all that Pieter might need, and his bed was in the one room, his table, his tools. What could be in the spare room?

But the lock would not turn.

She saw that a bird was at the window. She went to the window, and opened it, and the bird did not fly away, but stood quietly, peering at her.

—What is it you want? asked Elsbeth.

She fetched a crumb of cornbread from the table and gave it to the bird. It took the crumb up in its beak and flew away.

What then could that mean? asked Elsbeth, and she sat out on the front steps in the posture she had seen Pieter assume as he waited for her.

An hour passed, and she felt her worry returning. She must get back to the town. This was no place for her. The man was mad. He must be mad. She would not be here when the town sent men for Pieter.

Up she got, and into the house. From her dress she tore a piece, and she wrote on it,

----

Gone back to town. I will warn you before they come.
                              E.

She owed him that much at least.

And then she was out the door and across the field and on the road where night came to join her.

—Elsbeth! cried Catha, as she saw her sister at the door.

—Elsbeth, she said again. I have been waiting all night.

Elsbeth came into the room. She was filthy from head to foot from walking the dirt road. She was as weary as she'd ever been.

—I know, said Catha. I know where you went. It's plain on your face.

—It was a long walk, said Elsbeth.

—I will put water on for a bath. Change out of your clothes, and I'll set out some supper. Poor thing.

And so Catha filled a bath, and made a supper, and when Elsbeth emerged and sat down at table, she ate a little.

—Speak, said Catha, for I'll wait no more.

—I went to his house. He was there, alone, living alone. He has done . . . terrible things. He admitted as much, though he can't see it. He can't see what's wrong with the things he's done.

The sisters looked at each other as though from far away.

—Do you understand? asked Elsbeth.

—More and worse happened today, said Catha. There was another meeting. Loren, Malin's son, was out in a field. Malin said the field grew up around him and the boy was gone. Just like that, the boy gone. All the farmhands came, the field was searched clear from one end to the other, but the boy was gone.

—Cran's boy Levin Mills saw himself in a mirror, turned old, and when his sister found him, she couldn't comfort him. He's convinced his body's withering, and he can hardly draw a breath for fear.

—Dar Stane fell from a ladder, and his wife watching him. Fell to the street and landed on his head.

—Someone set fire to the Oulen's place. It near burned to the ground, and the barn as well, but the fire didn't touch the animals. They didn't even notice it.

—Ann Severn can't find her husband Tham. He went to gather wood, and hasn't been seen. There're a dozen stories, and a dozen more. People are angry. They're setting out in the morning to take him. Galvin Falk and twenty others. My Jaim spoke against it, but he was shouted down, and there wasn't much to say anyway, what with all that's been happening.

—Falk was angry, angry as I've ever seen him. He said we could not stand to live with a murderer not fifteen miles away. He said that even if we did not judge

—Four people dreamed it the first night, and seven the next. Everyone in town has dreamed the same dream, said Catha.

—What was it? Did you?

—No, said Catha. They dreamed of a wasteland, stretching into distance on all sides. At the center, a thin wooden ladder ascending out of sight through the clouds.

—But there's this, said Catha. Of all in the town, only one was brave enough to climb the ladder, even in a dream.

—Who? asked Elsbeth.

—Dunough Lark. She climbed it hand over hand, and when she passed through the first cloud, she said there was a world in red, that frightened her. When she passed through the second, there was a world in blue that gave her a sadness she will never dispel. Yet when she passed through the third, she found herself in her own room, made lovelier and stranger than she ever had been.

—And was it true?

—None would have recognized her, but for her voice, which was the same, but quieted.

When Elsbeth woke it was well past noon.

—Have they left? she cried, and she knew that they had, that the mayor's party had passed out along the road at first light.

Down the stairs she went. Jaim was there. He called out to her, but she ran on. On she went to the stable, where she hired a horse.

—Where is it you're going, Mistress Grimmer? asked the stablehand.

But Elsbeth rode past him without a word.

Out onto the road and urging the horse on. She was a quarter of the way there, then more, when she heard a pounding of hooves ahead on the road. She drew off, dismounted, and led her horse into the woods.

In the world, there is a time when one feels a confederacy with others. That time may last a short while. It may last through all of one's life. Elsbeth had felt that twice in this world, once with her sister, in a lasting bond, and once with Pieter. So unlike the others was she that she felt sometimes incapable even of speaking when out in public. The matter of greeting those who greet in the road was a huge complication, and she would go backways through the streets to avoid it. As a child, she had pretended there were two of her, Elsbeth, her parent's daughter, and Elsbeth-made-of-shadows. Elsbeth-made-of-shadows could do what she liked, and did. It was she who befriended Pieter. The things they did were not good things, not always. Once, they cut off a horse's hoof for no reason at all, and left it on the steps of the church.

Pieter was caught for that, but he did not say who had been with him, and Elsbeth had gone unpunished.

They had whipped and whipped him for that. Meyer the cart-driver, whose horse it was, was given way, and he had taken it.

The boy'd been held down by his father while Meyer laid into him. Elsbeth had watched, along with others.

How could they decide, she'd wondered, a penalty for the cutting off of a horse's hoof? Who is smart enough in this world to know what that crime equals, to know

Off the road, then, Elsbeth drew. She pushed the horse further, and turned to look back.

Movement and dust. Along then, the mayor's party, some twenty strong, riding slowly. Two and two carried a long pole, the mayor at the head, and from the pole hung a body, beaten and broken. On the pole a body hung. It was Pieter, stripped to his waist, slack with his mouth agog, chest blooded.

Falk's face was triumphant. He was a large man, and he wore his happiness openly now. He did not look to left or right, or he would have felt Elsbeth's eyes bore into him.

—You've killed him.

She dropped the reins and stepped forward.

Then the pole flickered. It flickered, and there was no one there, the horsemen were carrying an empty pole. She blinked and looked back. Pieter was again strung on the pole, slack in death, and then the horsemen were gone out of sight.

What was that? she wondered.

And a strange feeling made her say, I will continue to his house, to see what they have done.

The horse was waiting deeper in when she went to fetch him. He looked at her with his long horse eyes, and she felt that someone was looking through the horse's eyes, that someone could see her there where she was. She pulled the horse's head away from her, but it strained and turned and again it was looking at her.

—Come now, she said. Come along.

She rode on, but slower, and after a little while, came to where the road rose to overlook Pieter's holding. The line of trees wound like bunching thread up and around, holding the hill in a green fist, and there,

there, the house was burned to the ground. Where she had sat yesterday was ashes. She rode closer, and as she rode, the house flickered, flickered and was there.

She urged her horse on. Smoke was coming from the chimney. The door was opening. Pieter was alive. She was sure.

Elsbeth climbed down from the horse and ran up to the steps.

—Pieter, she called. Pieter!

—Elsbeth, said Pieter. Did I not tell you there was no worry here?

—But, I saw you, she said. I saw you on the pole.

—Some other man. Without luck. Perhaps not so clever as I.

—I saw you. It was you.

Pieter looked down at his feet.

—Those who came, said Pieter, felt they put me on the pole, felt they took me with them. They have seen my house burn. They have shown themselves to be that which they hate, that which they want to chase away out of the village. Well, there is a visiting that proceeds, that has proceeded this week in the town. Someone has been visiting, has he not?

Elsbeth was looking at her Pieter and her eyes were shining.

—I am glad, she said, that you are not on that pole. Whatever it means.

—Come and sit, said Pieter, for there was a supper laid out on the table. I will tend to your horse.

And he went out the door and down the steps. Through the window she could see his head laid against the

horse's head, though she could not hear his speaking
there.

What is it you have to say to horses at evening? What
understanding have you made?

She troubled him again and again with questions. How is it she had seen him on the pole. But he would say nothing about it, and would turn silent and cold, so she left off.

I will know in time all this, she thought.

And then Pieter was again with her, and serving the meat, which was a pale red meat, like venison. He had bread he'd baked, butter, cheese and fresh milk. She ate with a hunger she had never felt, ate and ate. Pieter ate too, and between them, they ate all that had been laid upon the table.

He showed her a silver glove he had made from the thinnest links.

—One wears it in the first hour of dawn, and chance goes a little ways with you on the road.

Scarcely do I believe it, thought Elsbeth,

and Pieter smiled.

From a hollow place in the wall he took out a long crook. It was reddish in color, with streaks of white.

—Have you sheep? she asked.

—I have had sheep, he said, though none now.

The door to the outside was open and a cat came in. Behind it was another cat and another.

—These go everywhere together, said Pieter. For they each know what's best for one of the others, but never for themselves.

He gave Elsbeth a bowl and she poured milk for the cats and laid it on the ground.

Elsbeth followed him in. He lit a candle and another and another, and the room was full of light.

What can be said of that room? There was a bed placed, as the others, in one wall. There was a broad window, widest of the house, looking out over the hill away from the road.

But most stirring, most unforeseen, most impossible of all, at the center of the room was an enormous loom, the best she had ever seen.

It was rooted to the ground upon legs like the legs of a young animal, sure in its strength. Its frame rose up, figured and etched. The wood was ebony, ebony all through.

—It can't be, said Elsbeth. It's made from a single piece of wood.

—It was brought here for you, said Pieter, many years ago, by a young man, building a house from his thought and wishes. He considered that perhaps Elsbeth might come one day out along the low road.

Then he brought out a bottle of warm drink, and they drank a glass together, and he left Elsbeth to her room, and left, closing the door.

And the first part of the night she spent running her

What can be said of waking in that house? That the dreams of the night before stood in turn to be examined, waiting with a patience unheard of?

Elsbeth remembered first:

A word learned by listening every day for years at a hole in the ground. Years and years passing and finally the word is said.

Then, all the through the town, all through the world one goes and no one can stand against one. The word is said, and houses are laid upon their sides, clouds form into veins that carry sight farther and farther than ever before. Can you see? asked the dream, the true depth of sight when one abandons the direction of one's life and takes to a single task, takes to listening at a hole in the ground, years and years, and finally a word is said?

That was the first dream.

The second:

A room full of coats. A coat of bird feathers, a coat that is the skin of a man, a coat that is the skin of a bear, the scales of a fish, the skin of a cat, of a mouse, of a snake, of a mule.

Then out that room and into another, where three suns rise in the farther sky. Men devoid of color sit playing at chess on a hundred tables. The pieces move untouched from square to square, and smoke rises from the ground where feet touch.

—There is no dust here, says the man who stands directly behind and cannot be seen.

—Do you know what that means, for there to be a place without dust?

The third:

A grand theatre, built to hold an audience of all that were ever born and all that will ever die, but the arriving there has taken place far too soon, and no one has come. Then, the wandering up and down aisles, empty aisles, the choosing of a seat from thousands made thousands in the thousandth part. Balconies, boxes, side-seats, hiding places on the roof, stools set on the stage-side, chairs built into the machinery of the lamps and bells and curtains.

Alone there and walking and walking, sitting first in one chair and then another, whistling and singing. Speaking first softly, and afterwards with a loud voice, for it is no matter. No one has come. One is far too early for the proceeding of life, even in one's own body.

To arrive too early even to live in one's own body.

And then sleep again.

That was the third dream.

The fourth dream:

As though in morning, with little warning, a yellow-haired man came in through the window.

Pieter Emily rose in his small room. In his house there were but two rooms. He went into the other and lit the stove. The yellow-haired man was already there.

The yellow-haired man was standing at once in all the rooms of the house, standing at once in every field, upon every roof, sitting in the boughs of every tree, prone upon each running stream, each still lake.

You cannot escape me, said the yellow-haired man.

But all at once, there were two countries, then three, then four, then five, and Pieter Emily and his cottage were nowhere to be found, and search as the sun might, its rays were like arms without hands, and could not lift the earth to see what lay beneath.

That was the fourth dream.

Yes, Elsbeth woke and looked about her. The room was there, with the full light pouring through the windows, and the loom at the room's center, strung like a harp, finer than ever. She sat at it, and felt the shuttle and how it sat upon her hand.

Then a knocking at the door.

—Elsbeth, will you come?

She rose and went to the door. Pieter was there.

—I must speak with you, he said.

Then they walked together the length of the house.

—Elsbeth Grimmer, said Pieter, and he looked at her but said no more.

He wants me to live here, thought Elsbeth.

And she thought of the loom, and how she had never seen a loom so fine. She thought of the feel of the place, like a house in a well to which no one can ever come. She could live here, she thought, and pass her days in weaving just as she would in town.

—Do you like the loom? he asked.

And she felt the truth of it. To leave her sister's house, to leave her shop, to leave the town . . . She could.

Elsbeth opened one of the narrow windows and leaned

out so that the land beyond was all about her, the hill and the house and the room behind.

I will live here, she thought to herself.

And Pieter nodded.

—You have had many dreams this night, said Pieter. If you like I will tell you the meaning of one, but only of one.

—This was the dream, said Elsbeth. I had lost my legs in a threshing accident, and instead of legs I wore long stilts buckled to my knees. On these stilts I could make speed through the fields and so I was a carrier of messages like no other. My father was a wealthy farmer, a prince of sorts, and all those merchants who came to him would speak and wonder at the beauty of his broken child fluttering above the wheat on legs of wood. Call to me, I would say, call to me, but none would call. None called, and when my father grew old, the farm was mine, and I wore a leather coat and carried a sling and kept a watch over the fields in the long night.

—What you invent, said Pieter, is as telling as a dream.

—Do you say so? asked Elsbeth.

—The threshing accident was birth, the wooden legs the loom. Your father is the town, the messages the needs perceptible to you in thread. Those visitors are nothing, the mountains beyond. You have no hope of them, and never did. The leather coat, the sling, are a step with the left foot and the right as you come here to me to speak not in defense of myself, but to protect your childhood which seems now so far.

—And yet, said he, it is the good fortune I have awaited, so we shall call it what you like.

The day was early still, and the sun beneath its zenith. Pieter and Elsbeth went to the hill's edge, where there was a well and a stone wall. The grass on either side of the stone wall was alike. It began and ended with no purpose.

—What is the purpose of this wall? asked Elsbeth.

—I built this wall, said Pieter, twenty years ago when I built the house, thinking of the day when we would walk out from the house and need a place to sit as I told you the necessities of your return.

Elsbeth smiled a smile of not-believing.

Then Pieter sat in a way that said, you need not believe me, but still it is true.

—You'll go then back to the town to fetch some things. But if you are to come and live here, you must obey these few things.

He looked sharply into Elsbeth's eyes.

—You must bring back no iron.

—You must say my name to no one, and say nothing of what you have seen.

—You must not sit in a chair or upon the ground when you are again in the town. Neither can you take food or drink.

224

—You must return here before the sun goes down, and you must bring back no more than you can carry in a single bag. There will be a new life for you here, with as many things as you desire. These things that you will bring will be the last of your old life.

Elsbeth nodded.

—And you must not be cut, or let a drop of blood out of you in the town. There is time still today. Go and return.

Elsbeth stood.

—I will bring no iron, she said. I will sit nowhere. I will say nothing of what I have seen. I will take no drink, no food. I will return before sunset, and I will take but a single bag. No blood will come from me while I am in the town.

Pieter wore a long coat of harsh canvas, buttoned on the side, and he had at his side a long knife.

—What will you do, asked Elsbeth, while I am gone?

—I'll check on my field, give food to my animals, and set out in the woods.

—You must be here when *I* return, said Elsbeth.

—Have no fear of that, said Pieter, for I know every way in the wood, and can judge time from the limbs of trees.

Then they were parted, and Elsbeth rode away into the town, and when she looked back from a rise in the road what she saw behind her was a burned-out cottage on a ravaged hill, and she found that her clothes were dirty, as though she had slept the night on a bed of ashes.

After a short ride, Elsbeth reached the town. She saw it from a distance, its intricacy of wood and walkways, its rising of turrets and workshops. Smoke rose from dozens of chimneys, people leaned out windows. The warmth of the sun was here though it had not been with them on the hillside at the reasonless wall.

—Will I go back? asked Elsbeth. And then she thought of the loom, and her blood stirred.

I can, she thought, always return to the town one day. If I like, I can return after a month, after a week. I need not stay with Pieter forever.

But she saw in his face a hardness and she knew that what was binding to him would be binding to her.

At the stable she left the horse, and went on home.

Moll Ongar stopped her at a crossing.

—Elsbeth, she cried out. Elsbeth have you heard?

—What is it, Moll?

Moll's face was red with the news.

—The mayor, squeaked Moll, Falk's hand was cut off at the wrist. He reached into a cupboard and when he pulled his arm out there was blood everywhere. I mean, they brought in the body of Pieter Emily today, and hung it on the gate. I said so myself, I said it was bad luck, and now see what's happened.

—Where is the body? asked Elsbeth.

—The main gate.

Elsbeth stood looking up at the arch. There was blood there, where the hook was, but no body.

Took him down an hour ago.

—What?

Elsbeth turned.

—What did you say?

An old man was sitting there in the shade.

—I said they took him down an hour ago. I've been sitting here all day. I watched them bring him, watched them hang him up, and I watched them come an hour ago, take him down and drag him off to burial.

—Where would that be? asked Elsbeth.

—Where do you suppose? asked the old man.

He spat on the ground.

—I don't know, said Elsbeth, the graveyard?

—Would you want him there? asked the old man, with decent folk?

Elsbeth narrowed her eyes.

—Where are they burying him?

—Why do you care anyway? said the man suspiciously.

Another old man came out of the inn and sat down on the bench next to the first old man.

What's the news? he said.

—This woman's wanting to know where they took Jansen's son.

—Jansen's son?

—Yeah, where they took him.

—Doesn't she know that?

—Seems not.

The second old man looked up at Elsbeth.

—Haven't seen you in a time, he said. Elsbeth Grinner. My son says the shops been closed last few days.

—Clef Carr, tell me this minute, said Elsbeth. Where is Pieter Emily being buried?

—Buried him already, said Carr. In a plot by the church, face down like a suicide, from shame.

No one was at the house when she arrived. Elsbeth went up to her room and laid out a bag. She changed her dirty dress for another, and filled the bag with a few things, then a few more. She set out all she'd like to take with her, and saw that it was more than would fit in the one bag.

—I could take two, she said. Two would not be so bad. He couldn't object to two.

But when she left the room, it was with the one bag, and having left the best of her things behind.

On the stairs, she heard the door creak. Catha came in.

—Elsbeth, she said. Elsbeth, where have you been?

And Elsbeth looked at her and said nothing.

—Elsbeth, she said, where have you been?

—I went, said Elsbeth, to the mountain pass, to see if it's clear, to see if anyone come from the outside.

Catha shook her head.

—That's a lie, she said. What are you doing with that sack? Where are you going now all dressed to travel?

Elsbeth looked at her feet.

—What's going on? said Catha. Last night I dreamt the strangest dreams, so clear I could remember all when I

—I dreamed of a opera house like the ones in the great cities of the East, a grand place, as large as a city itself, and made to hold all that were ever born, or ever will be. Yet it was morning, and the opera is an evening's word. It was morning and I came there all alone to walk among the seats as through a forest of pines, where the needles make a bed and all's quiet. There were no hands to hold, and so I held my own and went through the arcades, the balconies, the anterooms, calling out, but no one came. The roof of the opera was painted like the sky, and changed like the sky, changing as I moved, and ceasing when I ceased. All the lights were lit, great lamps burning at every interval, in every unpeopled room. I felt that you were there, that you had been there.

Said Elsbeth,

—I was there, with you, and you with me, but we could be no comfort to each other.

—And this? asked Catha, her hand taking in the sack, the traveling clothes.

—There's no comfort for me here, said Elsbeth, only craft and continuing.

—Do you know, said Catha, taking her sister in an embrace, that they killed him?

Catha began to cry.

—They killed him, she said, and hung him on the gate.

To this Elsbeth said nothing.

—Where have you been? asked Catha. Oh, you will not tell me. Then go, and go, and I shall watch you from behind your shoulder, as I always have.

—And I you, said Elsbeth.

On the stoop she set down her sack, for a thought had pricked her. What of iron had she taken unwittingly?

And from her sack she drew a penknife, from her sack she drew three needles, from her sack she drew a scissor, all gone there unknown.

She left these on the doorstep, and made to go. But Catha called to her from the door.

—Are you not hungry? Let me make you a meal before you go. Let us sit and have a drink.

And in Elsbeth then a hunger greater than she had ever felt. Yet she dismissed it. Then in Elsbeth a thirst as for the sea.

He said *no food and drink*. To have one drink alone . . . It might be all right. She went into the house, and Catha poured a glass and a glass of wine.

—Sit, said Catha.

—Oh, said Elsbeth, I cannot.

And she turned away from her sister, standing there with the two glasses.

—Goodbye.

Then she fled through the door, and as she did a nail caught at her.

Her sleeve tore and the nail was against her skin. But it did not cut.

Elsbeth breathed and closed her eyes.

—Goodbye, she said again.

And then she was out in the day and the day was soon to finish. Bag over her shoulder, she made her way down to the stable. I will go another way, she thought, than the usual. I do not want to see anyone at all.

So she took the alley behind the main street, and went along behind shops and houses. As she drew near the stable and the town's edge, a voice called out.

—Elsbeth. Elsbeth Grinner.

She turned. It was the priest.

—Father, she said.

—My daughter, what ails you?

He came up, Father Rutlin, and took her chin in his hand.

—What ails you? he said.

—I am as well as I may be, said Elsbeth.

She tried to pull away, but he would not let her.

—Elsbeth, he said, Elsbeth, there is a skin on you. Another skin, that you cannot see.

He ran his hand over her face and along her arm.

—There is another skin. It is between you and the world. I shall take it away.

—No, said Elsbeth. Do nothing!

But Rutlin held his hands at her temples and spoke beneath his breath, and when he let her go, he drew something off her that left her weak in the legs and arms.

—Come tomorrow, said Rutlin, I demand it.

And he fixed her with his eye.

The light of the sun was lying on its side and coming here and there through the houses and walls.

Elsbeth looked helplessly back and then broke away.

—Elsbeth, he called. Come tomorrow. Heed me.

On down the road on horse, on horse down the low road as the road sank and the sun sank, and a weight was upon her.

He must let me in, she thought. He must.

On she went, and evening drew near. Yet as she came down the side of the last hill, the sun was in the sky, still above the trees.

I am in time, she thought, and she urged the horse on.

The cottage appeared before her in ashes, as it had been. It lay ahead, in ashes. Up the hill she came, and down from the horse. The cottage was in ashes.

—Change, she thought. Change. Flicker and be here.

But she came on horse, and then she came on foot to the cottage, and the ground was ash. The cottage was ash. She walked about in the ashes, and moved them with her feet. The horse went off to graze where it had been the morning before. And the sun was gone from the sky, and she laid down in the ash and wept, and fell into sleep, and this is what she dreamed:

She was sitting at the loom, the black loom, strung as it had been by her the night before. She began to weave, and she wove faster and faster, and the room began to spin. She wove and she wove and a pattern grew, and she could see what it was in the pattern, rising from her hand.

A red blot growing, and then it was a fox, and a wood grew about it, and hills, and a road. A party of horsemen could be seen, and a pole they were carrying, a man hung from it. In the distance, a town of wood, a box of wood, a town like a box of wood. Three suns in the sky, each weaker than the one before. And at the edge of the town, a man with a woman's skin in his hand. Then the loom cracked in half and broke to the floor, and Elsbeth woke.

the early deaths of
lubeck, brennan,
harp & carr

2006

Four of them were on one side of a dim room.

—I'm going to try it, said the first.

The girl watched herself in the mirror as the young man approached.

—I wonder, he said. I thought perhaps . . .

He stopped mid-sentence, for tears had begun to well up out of the girl's eyes. She began to cry.

—Please, she said, just leave me alone.

She wore a straight brown dress, buttoned all up the side, and a long tweed coat. Her hair was braided into itself.

—Are you all right? he asked. Can I help you?

—You know, you can't just speak to people. That's not how things are anymore. No one wants to just be spoken to.

She rubbed her eyes.

—It's rather silly of you. Already you look a bit like a fool.

The barkeeper, standing just across the bar, nodded.

—There are rules, he said.

And indeed, on the wall, a list of rules.

—I'm sorry. I didn't know.

—That's no excuse.

The girl stood up as if to go.

—I'll take care of this, Myrna, said the barkeeper. You stay where you are.

He came around the bar towards Harp. He was a big man, with thick forearms like a steelworker.

—It's time for you to go, lad. The others too.

—Come on, said Harp, taking a step back. The place is empty. I'll just go back to the table. We'll mind our own business.

—Hey, Barton! the man called to the back.

Another man appeared.

—Get out.

Harp's friends had come over.

—What's the problem? said Lubeck.

—The lot of you, said the barkeeper. Get out.

—We didn't do anything, said Carr. Why should we leave? Our money's good.

The girl spoke up.

—He told me if I didn't go into the back with him he'd hit me. He said he was going to take me off somewhere and tear me in half. Wouldn't think nothing of it, he said. Just like that.

Her face was fierce and covered in tears.

—What? I didn't . . .

The barkeeper and the man called Barton looked at each other.

Barton grabbed Harp and lifted him from the ground. At a sort of half run, he went for the door and heaved him through.

The barkeeper took Brennan's shoulder. Brennan wrenched away, and ran for the door past Barton. It was a general flight.

—If I ever see you in here again, said the barkeeper.

Harp's face was bruised and cut from the street where he'd been thrown. They dusted him off and continued.

—What was that?

—Why did she say that?

—Who was that girl?

They soon came to another place and began again. Lubeck was talking to two dressed like match-stick girls.

—Can you believe it?

—That's ridiculous, said the first girl. She must have a score to settle, and she can't settle it.

—I don't know, said the second girl. Maybe you deserved it. I don't know.

Lubeck spoke up.

—But Harp didn't say anything like that. The girl just invented it. She made it all up.

—Well it had to come from somewhere, didn't it, said the second match-stick girl. It had to come from somewhere.

—That's right, said the first match-girl. Even if she was making it up.

—But it's not fair, said Carr. She made the whole thing up. It wasn't true.

—Well, I guess you're right then, said the second match-stick girl. But any way you look at it, you lost. If she wasn't lying, well then, your friend deserved what he got, and it was her speaking up that caused him to get punished, in which case she won, and if she *was* lying, then she managed to trick those guys into throwing you out, in which case she still won. She won and you lost, and it was the four of you against just her. That's pretty good.

The match-stick girls agreed: the girl in the brown dress had won.

An hour or two went by.

It was thus late in the evening when one of the match-stick girls yelped.

—Hey, isn't that the girl. Isn't that her out the window?

—That's her, said Harp. Damned if it isn't her. Let's go.

—What'll we do? asked Carr.

—I don't know, said Harp. Let's go.

The party poured out into the street, with the four young men out ahead of the others. Indeed, the long tweed coat and brown dress of the girl could be made out just up ahead. It had snowed the day before, and drifts and piles lined the street. The girl walked there in the company of an older man.

—Let's pelt them, said Harp.

He forced the brown, gritty snow into a ball as the others did the same. Then with a shout, they ran forward, throwing the snowballs as hard as they could.

The first missed the man's shoulder by an arm's length. But the second struck him. He turned, face lit up with anger. The girl stopped too, and turned, and just at the moment, a snowball struck her hard in the face. In the moment before it struck a fact became plain to all of them:

It was not the girl, but someone else, a woman of perhaps forty.

She tumbled down falling heavily onto her back with a cry. The man started after them. What was there to do? They ran. Down the first alley, onto the next street, a right turn, a left, onto another street, onto another alley. They were young and in good health, and so they made it safely away.

the second

Carr woke to banging on the door to his flat. He pulled on a pair of pants and went to see what it was.

It was Harp.

—You've got to come with me. It's bad. Come to Lubeck's place.

Lubeck and Brennan, two of the four young men, lived near the river in a big house run by Lubeck's mother.

—Give me a second, said Carr.

He finished dressing and then the two were walking in the street.

—What is it?

—Lubeck got a letter. You'll see.

More than that, Harp wouldn't say.

It was Lubeck's mother let Carr in. Brennan came to the door too. Lubeck was sitting in a chair by the window.

—What is it? asked Carr. What happened?

Brennan took a letter off a side table and handed it to Carr.

—Read it for yourself, he said.

DEAR J. LUBECK,
It is my understanding that you and three others, L. Carr, F. Brennan, and J. Harp, were on Sycamore Street last night where I went walking with my wife. You must understand that we were at the hospital much of the night. My wife has been caused to have a miscarriage. While I might take this matter up with the police, I prefer, as a gentleman, to meet with you and decide the matter by force. Your family has long lived in this town, and so I believe you will honor your commitment. Come then, tomorrow morning, that is, 5 Dec., to the racing track out past Elridge green no later than 6 a.m. Bring a second, as I shall.

most sincerely,
Judge Allen Henry

—Believe it, said Lubeck's mother.

She called to Lubeck from across the room.

—You won't fail us, will you, John?

—There's nothing to do, said Lubeck, standing up, still looking out the window. There's nothing to do.

—That's right, said his mother. It's the only thing.

She looked them one by one, Brennan, Carr, Harp, full in the face.

—A thing like that, she said. It's awful. There's no choice in the matter. You've got to have it out or we can't live in this town.

Lubeck's brothers and sisters had come into the room. There were perhaps eight of them of various sorts and ages. Lubeck's stepfather also had come in.

—A bad business, a bad business, he said, and pulled at his moustache. Seems to me you deserve what you get.

—That's right, said Lubeck's mother.

—These days, what with automobiles and propeller airplanes, the power of man is getting stronger and stronger, said Lubeck's stepfather. If he doesn't learn some moral strength, it'll all be as unjointed as a scarecrow.

—I don't even know what you're saying, said Lubeck.

—Suit yourself, said Lubeck's stepfather.

—This is a very very bad thing, said Brennan.

—It's a very bad thing, all right, said Lubeck's mother.

The next morning, Carr went with Lubeck. Brennan had refused, and though Harp had wanted to come, Lubeck wouldn't have it.

—You've got to come along, Lubeck had told Carr. Just you.

They took Lubeck's stepfather's automobile, and drove out from the town. The morning light where the snow still held was strong in their eyes, and they squinted as they came.

Soon they reached the track. A car could be seen through the bare trees, and a few figures beside it.

Lubeck pulled in and stopped the engine.

—The pistols are there, the man said.

He was as old as the Judge. Both wore overcoats over dark suits. Both wore hats and thin leather gloves. They had laid a soft cloth over a portion of the car's hood. On the cloth were two revolvers. The scene was very dignified. One would want, as a child, to be old enough to take part in such a thing, to be there in the heaving coldness of morning, in the careful grace of winter, though of course, the true penalty of death cannot be considered in its depth by such a little fool as a child. No, no.

—Either, said the Judge.

—What?

—You can take either.

The Judge's second walked out and drew two lines in the earth of the cinder track, about twenty feet apart. He called Carr over.

—The way this thing is going to get done, well, this is it. Lubeck and Judge Henry will wait, each some yards behind their line. At our word, each approaches his line. When the line is reached, they begin to fire.

—How many shots can they . . . ?

—Eight in each revolver. If they both run out, we start again.

He looked at Carr with disgust.

—You were with him, weren't you? You're one of them?

—I, well . . .

The man turned his back on Carr and approached the place where the Judge was waiting.

—All set, he said.

Judge Henry motioned to Lubeck to take a pistol from the hood. Lubeck hesitated, then chose, lifting the gun uncertainly.

Carr was at his side. They took a few steps together away from the others.

—You can leave. You don't have to do this, he said quietly. Leave the town. Leave the country.

Lubeck looked at him and away.

—Tell them I'm ready.

—To your posts, said the Judge's second.

The Judge and Lubeck stepped out onto the track.

Carr felt as if someone were squeezing all the air out of his body. Things became slow and strained. He heard the man call "NOW!" and watched as Lubeck and the Judge advanced, step by step. Near the lines, they raised their pistols. They pointed their pistols at each other. Carr couldn't breathe. He was held there, without breath, as the shots began. Lubeck fired and fired. The Judge fired, fired again. Both continued advancing. The noise was incredible. He felt he had never heard anything so loud. Lubeck fired and the Judge flinched, and then they were just walking at each other, just walking. The Judge let out three shots in a row. The shots just poured from his revolver. Lubeck was not firing. His face was turned away. The first shot came. The second shot came. The third shot came, and Lubeck was backwards off his feet.

Carr ran out onto the track. He slowed his pace as he drew closer. The bullet had taken Lubeck high in the cheek and gone straight through his head. The face was a bloody wreck. He was no longer there.

Carr realized he had started to breathe again. He turned. The Judge and his second were conferring. The second came over, passed Carr, knelt by Lubeck's body. He was taking the pistol back. He removed the pistol from Lubeck's hand, opened it, dropped the spent shells on the ground, and walked away.

Then he paused.

—You, he said. Give this to Brennan.

He was holding a letter.

Across the length of track, the Judge was looking straight into Carr's eye. His face was carved like a mask of a face.

Carr drove very gently along the road. He had found soft leather driving gloves on the dash and he had put them on and now he was driving gently. He negotiated one turn then another. He was bringing Lubeck's mother her son's body. Such a thing he had never done, but he felt it was within him to do it.

Lubeck was stretched out in the back seat. Carr had wrapped his head in a sack. Other than that, he might have been asleep. One often, however, can take the sign of a bag over a person's head to mean that something bad has either happened or will happen. So, anyone observing the scene would not have to wonder for very long at the difficulties that were assailing young Carr as he drove gently on the twisting road back into town.

Over a small bridge and down by the harbor. Along an alley and stopped beside a huge oak. Then, to the door.

Come out, he said. *Come out.*

They came out, many of them, a crowd of them, all down to the road where Lubeck was. Carr went gently away.

Do you know the surface of the stream? Do you know its depth? Do you see as fish see, that water is not one but many, that there are paths through it, just as through land, and that to pass along a stream is a matter well beyond the powers of any human being?

Carr was reading from a thin book. He was still near the harbor, on a bench. He felt that he could not leave without giving Brennan the letter. But he did not want to.

A little girl was there with a cygnet on a narrow leather leash. She drew near and looked at Carr. Carr looked at her.

—When it grows up, it will do its best to hurt you, he said. I know that much.

—Her name is Absinthe, said the girl. And I'm Jane Charon.

—Nice to meet you, Jane.

—Not so nice for me, said Jane stoutly. You say such horrible things.

—I saw a swan maul a child once, said Carr. The child had to be removed. To the hospital, I mean. The swan was beaten to death with a stick.

Jane covered the cygnet's ears. You'll have to imagine for yourself what that looked like. I don't really know where a bird's ears are.

—But, said Jane. If you were there, why didn't you help the child?

—Sometimes, when you see something awful about to happen, although you are a good person and mean everything for the best, you hope still that the bad thing will happen. You watch and hope that the awful thing will happen and that you will see it. Then when it happens you are surprised and shocked and pretend about how you didn't want it to happen. But really you did. It was that way with me and the swan.

—So, you were on the swan's side? asked Jane.

—I guess so. Yes, that's right.

—Well, that's even worse. It's all right for a person to pick a side, but once he's on that side he should stay there. You ought to have helped the swan escape. You should have stopped them from killing it, and helped it away. Or even helped it to maul the child, if you were really the swan's friend. How could anyone ever trust you?

Jane gave Carr a very stern look and continued on down the path. The cygnet nipped at him as it passed, but its beak got fouled up in Carr's coat, and it missed.

—You can't own a swan, anyway, Carr yelled, somewhat spitefully. The Queen of England owns them all already.

And it was true. The Queen of England is the owner of all swans. It was decided a long time ago, and so it has always been.

THE LETTER

The letter was in a cream-colored envelope. Francis Brennan, it said on the outside.

Carr gave the envelope to Brennan. He was standing on the stairs. Then he was handing the envelope to Brennan.

—What is this? said Brennan.

—They gave it to me. This morning, they gave it to me, for you.

Brennan took the envelope reluctantly. He turned it over in his hand.

—Tell me how it happened, he said.

—He shot Lubeck, and then they gave me the envelope. That's it.

—That's it, said Brennan.

He opened the envelope.

The floor of the room was wooden, and the boards ran for a very long way. Carr saw the board all the way to the wall and then back.

Brennan handed the opened letter back to Carr.

—What's there to do? said Brennan.

He was a man of some principle, Brennan. He was studying for a Doctorate in Philosophy, and believed in maintaining a certain decorum in one's manner of life. Nevertheless, he had refused to go with Lubeck that morning, and now he was to go himself.

—You'll go with me, won't you? he said to Carr.

—I will, said Carr, feeling the massive unbowed hand of fate upon his shoulder.

A long pause, then:

—Was he a very good shot? asked Brennan.

—Rather not. They were pretty close, and firing and firing. He must have missed Lubeck six or seven times.

He did not say anything about how Lubeck had stopped firing. He felt it might make matters worse.

—Six or seven times, said Brennan to himself. Six or seven times. At how many paces?

—Paces? I don't know about paces. It was about twenty feet, though closer when he shot him.

Brennan nodded.

—Twenty feet.

It mustn't have seemed to Brennan that the Judge was a very good pistoleer. However, the fact of the matter is, it is not so easy to shoot someone with a gun, even when you want to. In the Great War, for instance, people were always shooting their guns in the air instead of at the enemy.

—I'm going to just be here, said Brennan.

—All right.

—I'll just be here, all right?

—All right. And I'll meet you here.

—Here's fine.

So, Carr left. Outside it was already dark and quite cold. Certain patches of air were colder than others, for there was no wind at all, none. He walked through these various patches and thought all the while of the soft cloth on which the pistols had been laid.

THE CLOTH

At that exact moment, the cloth was wrapped about both pistols in an intricate way so that the pistols were both protected from each other, and from outside objects. The pistols had been taken apart, cleaned and oiled, and put back together. Now, they sat in the trunk of the Judge's automobile. The automobile was in the drive before the Judge's house. The Judge was inside, sitting with his wife. She was pleading with him.

Carr could not sleep. He tried to read, but couldn't make sense of anything. Then, he thought,

perhaps if I sit at the table, which is bare, I will be able to think of something that will put me in a position to sleep.

Often, I think, when one can't sleep it is because one is, of a sudden, required to come to a certain conclusion or think through a certain idea, and one is unable to do it. Only by sheer exhaustion, deception, or pharmaceuticals, can one pass by.

He sat at the table.

The ancient Egyptians believed that there was a traveler, a god who was a traveler, who would come sometimes to table. You would never know him. He would just come knocking at your door, begging a meal, and if you let him in and fed him, if you gave him a place to stay, and kindness, he would reward you by teaching you the language that cats speak, so that, when you were dead, you could listen and learn from them the passage to paradise.

Lubeck was never kind, thought Carr. If anyone ever came begging at his door, he did not let that person in.

Brennan was waiting on the steps when Carr arrived. Lubeck's stepfather came out. He gave Brennan a key.

—There's not much to know anyway, he said. It all just continues.

Brennan stood up.

—Let's go, he said.

Carr nodded to Lubeck's stepfather. Then away.

It was the same automobile. The bag had not stopped all the blood from coming out of the head the day before, and the back seat was stained.

—I'll drive, said Carr.

Brennan was singing beneath his breath. Carr could not make out what it was. They passed along the streets, over the bridge, out of the town, through fields on the raised road and, again, there loomed up the specter of the track, the car through the bare trees, the waiting men beside it.

—How did this happen, said Brennan quietly.

—It's happening, said Carr.

—What's right? said Brennan. If I kill him, then his wife will have lost her husband and her child.

—You can't think about that, said Carr.

—Maybe I'll shoot him in the leg, said Brennan. Then it'll stop.

The pistols were laid out on the hood again, on the same cloth.

Which one did Lubeck take? whispered Brennan.

—I don't remember, said Carr. They look the same.

—They are the same, said the Judge's second.

—They are not the same, said Brennan. One worked yesterday, and the other didn't.

—Are you saying that . . . ? began the Judge's second.

—No, no. I'm sure both revolvers fired, and accurately. That's not what I'm saying. But one *worked*. Which one was it?

The Judge heard the argument and came over.

—What's the trouble, he asked.

—He wants to know which gun was yours.

The Judge pointed to the left one. Brennan took it.

The marks were still on the track from the day before, but the Judge's second redrew them anyway, with a broken stick. He smoothed over the place where Lubeck fell. He motioned to Carr.

—This goes the same way.

—I've explained it to him, said Carr.

—Right.

Carr nodded to Brennan, who was holding the pistol in both his hands with the barrel pointed down. Brennan walked slowly to the line.

—No, said Carr. You have to be back a bit.

—Oh, said Brennan. I'm sorry, I forgot.

His hands were shaking.

The Judge stood well behind his line. He nodded to his second. His second nodded to Carr.

—Ready? Carr asked Brennan.

Brennan's face was curled up. He shook it a little, enough for a nod.

—Now.

The Judge advanced to his line.

Brennan stayed where he was.

The Judge raised the revolver and pointed it at Brennan. Brennan raised his pistol. He was still holding it with both hands. The gun shook uncontrollably.

—Come forward to the line, shouted the Judge's second.

—He's got to come forward, he said to Carr.

—Brennan, go to the line.

Brennan looked around uncertainly.

—To the line.

He started to walk forward, his pistol held out before him.

The Judge's gun was in line with Brennan. He held it carefully and squeezed.

The sound came and was gone. It seemed to pass along over the ground, to catch at Brennan and throw him down, and then disperse.

Brennan was coughing and holding his chest. Blood was all on his mouth. He kept wiping it away, but the mouth stayed bloody. There was always more blood and more blood on the mouth.

—Leon, he said. Leon.

Carr knelt by him. The bullet had entered Brennan's chest and pierced his lung. His mouth was full of blood.

Blood was on his face and neck, on his hands. He was still holding the pistol. Carr took it from him and put it on the ground.

—Frank, he said. Frank, you're all right.

—I'm all right, said Brennan.

—Just hold it together. We'll get you to a hospital.

—No one's getting to a hospital, said the Judge's second.

Carr stood up.

—He's had a bullet through his chest. Isn't that enough for you? I'm taking him to a hospital, and you won't stop me.

—I certainly will, said the Judge's second. He took the pistol up off the ground and held it very seriously in his hand.

A minute passed. Then another. Brennan's coughing was quieter now.

Carr started towards the car.

—I'm going to get help. I don't care what you say.

—It's useless to talk about it, said the Judge, approaching. He's dead already.

And indeed Brennan's chest had stopped moving.

—This, for you, said the second, handing Carr an envelope.

James Harp, it read.

All around them the morning squatted unwelcoming with long trails of foiling distance.

The Judge and his second were standing together and speaking quietly.

What could they possibly be saying?

—James, he said. JAMES, he said again, louder, banging on the door.

He could hear the sound of someone moving around inside.

—Harp, you bastard, open the door.

The door opened. Harp stood there in a dressing gown. He was a mess. His face was still swollen up.

—What do you want? he said.

—They're both dead.

—You think I don't know that?

Carr stood there. He couldn't say anything. He tried to, but he couldn't. He was just standing there, holding the envelope. He refused to look at it. He was not holding an envelope. He would not look at it.

He looked down at the envelope.

—What's that? said Harp.

—What?

—What are you holding? Carr, what's that in your hand?

Carr was standing there with the envelope after all. He handed it to Harp.

—It has my name on it. What, you were just standing there with an envelope with my name on it, and not saying anything? You got it from them, didn't you? They send you along each day, their messenger. What is that? If you were my friend, you'd have thrown it away. Now I have to see it. Now I have to do something.

—Well, do something, said Carr.

Harp tore open the envelope. A girl came out from his room.

—What's that? she said.

—Nothing, said Harp.

—Give me that, she said. Give it to me.

She tried to take the envelope from Harp. He twisted away. She tore it out of his hands and ran back into the room.

—Come back here!

Harp ran after. Carr followed.

There was a fireplace in the far corner. The girl was standing in front of it. The letter was gone.

—It doesn't make a difference, Alice.

—What do you mean? she said.

Harp said nothing.

—What does he mean?

—I don't know.

—You know, damn you. Tell me what he means.

—He means he knows what the letter said, even if he didn't read it. There's nothing to be done.

She shrieked and started pounding on Harp's chest and face with her hands.

—No! You're not going. You're not going.

Harp looked over her at Carr. His features had composed themselves.

—Tomorrow morning? he said.

Carr nodded.

Out on the street there was a dandy parade in progress. Little boys were dressed up in bright blue soldier suits and carrying little guns and swords and such. Others were with trumpets and bugles, some with drums. It was quite a clatter! There were adults too, in adult versions of the ridiculous child uniforms, walking at the front. There was a banner too, but the banner was already gone up ahead and Carr could not read what it said.

The parade was going in the direction that Carr needed to go.

Should I join the parade? he wondered.

That's always the decision one is pressed to make. Do I join the parade or not? In certain cases the decision is easy, in others not so.

Now there was a mule with a very small child on it dressed up also like a mule. Or rather like a monk in a hair suit.

A hair suit, thought Carr. I haven't seen one of those in a long time.

Yes, these and other thoughts of guilt.

After the mule came four dancers bent up and twisted onto each other to look like an elephant. They were very successful in this. I imagine they were the best ones in the world at being in a parade and looking like an elephant.

Even if everyone were to try to do it, they would still be the best, that's how good they were. I wouldn't want you to think that just because no one ever bothers trying to look like an elephant with other people together in a parade that these people being the best didn't mean much because certainly it did. They were very pleasant to look at, sort of dragging their way along the street. One had an arm to be the trunk, and it was painted gray like a trunk, and all the hair had been shaved from it. It moved back and forth the way an elephant trunk moves, always seeming like it was about to investigate some smell or shape. The people who made up this elephant were very determined. It must have hurt a great deal to go all the way through the town on the hard pavement.

And that was that about the elephant. Already it was gone.

Next came a group of little girls with pigeons on their shoulders. These were the kind that send messages. Apparently there was a society of girls that does this all the time. Although I have never seen them in action, I believe it to be true. Carr saw the society pass there, and immediately thought of a message he should like to send by pigeon. But, of course, the society was not accepting messages at that time.

When Carr finally got back to his house it was mid-afternoon. He sat on the floor and looked at the books piled up there.

In the evening, he told himself, I will go to a nice cafe and I will read straight through from beginning to end *Gargantua* in French. Then, someone will approach, a lovely girl most likely, and say, oh, do you like Rabelais, and I will say, well, sometimes, but just for light reading, and then I will take out a copy of Locke and pretend that I am a much more serious and orderly person than I actually am. Won't that go well for me.

In fact, at the cafe he read some Robert Louis Stevenson, who is not only for children, and this was very rousing, and he looked about himself with a bright strong gaze.

It did not seem possible to him that anything that was happening had actually happened or even could actually happen.

Is there to be a funeral, he wondered. Will their funerals be together? He said these things quietly to himself in such a way that they were not really questions. For he himself wondered if it was true as he felt that he was the fourth and that he would be the fourth. What, he wondered, would happen then?

Someone did approach him. It was a Prussian bandleader.

—Is there, said the man, some problem?

—No, said Leon Carr.

—Why have you been staring at me then?

—I'm sorry, said Carr. I have been thinking very hard about something.

—Ah, said the man. Well, I suppose it's all right then. All the same, I would rather you stop doing it. Will you stop?

—I'll try, said Carr. But it's a bit difficult, you see. You're sitting across from me. If I'm thinking, and looking in that direction, then you might feel I'm looking at you, even if I'm not.

The Prussian bandleader thought about this.

—This is why, he said, in Prussia, we don't allow people to sit opposite one another. It makes for fewer offenses.

—One can't believe a word you say, said Carr.

—There's not much courtesy in you, is there? said the Prussian. Goodnight.

He doffed his hat to Carr and went back to his seat. From time to time Carr was mindful of staring at the man, and at those times he looked away.

Carr was thinking of how he had imagined for himself a house with a long porch set on a small elevation above a street in a seashore town. He had joined a daydreaming league in the days when those things were popular, and when they would all lie together daydreaming, he would dream of this house. The particulars of each room were clear in his head. He would have bookshelves lining the staircases in the house. There would be many staircases, at least one for every room. Bathrooms would be gotten to via staircases, rooms would never be on the same elevation. In fact, the house would be a bit of a conundrum for the architect and engineer. He had often imagined explaining his creation. What an argument that would be. He had imagined his reply. *Spare no expense, my boys, spare no expense. I am prepared to pay handsomely.* And then everyone would be smiling and understanding each other.

It was freezing cold when he woke. He'd left the window open the night before. He limped across the floor, still draped in blankets, shut the window, and returned to bed. The sky outside was lightening.

I won't go, he thought to himself. I can just stay here. Or, I can get all my things together and leave. I'll go to another town. That wouldn't be so bad. Nothing keeps me here, really. There's no one for me here. I can go.

But Carr most of all felt the guilt of what they'd done, and Carr, of them all, was the last one who would ever run away.

I will run away, he thought.

He packed his things up hastily into a large suitcase. Then he stood looking down into it.

If I don't go now, I'll never be in time to meet Harp.

The door shut. The suitcase was still open on the floor, and Carr, coat in hand, ran down the stairs and out into the day.

He drew his hand back to knock, and the door opened. Harp was standing there, very neatly dressed. He looked quite determined. The girl Carr had seen the day before was there as well, to watch them go. She was not as wild as the day before.

—Goodbye, she said.

—Goodbye.

Harp shut the door.

—The car's in the side alley, he said.

Out the back way and into the alley. There was the car. Out the alley into the street. Along the street to the bridge. Across the bridge to the roads beyond. All down all down to the track, where, through bare trees, one could see a stopped car and figures waiting.

—Whatever happens, don't worry, said Harp. It'll all work out.

—What do you mean?

—Don't worry about what I mean. Don't worry about anything. Just keep clear.

—All right, said Carr.

They got out. Again, the Judge was standing with his second. Again the cloth was spread on the hood with the revolvers.

They approached.

The track was a long arc laid out to the side between craggy fists of trees and rising of hills. There were stands in the distance, and stables beyond the stands. Above the stands the sky seemed farther than it ought to be. What was the distance of the sky? Did it change from place to place? People thought once that heaven was somewhere beyond the moon. Everything was divided up that way. Some things were beneath the moon, others above. It meant something to be able to go beyond the moon.

The Judge's second was explaining about how Harp might use either of the revolvers. Harp was staring at the revolvers. He wasn't saying anything, just staring.

—Harp. Harp. Hey, Harp, said Carr.

He felt that something was wrong.

—Harp!

Harp looked up suddenly. He was standing with his back to Carr. The Judge and his second were frozen.

—What's the meaning of this?

—I'm not going to die, not today, said Harp.

—What are you doing? shouted Carr.

There was an automatic pistol in Harp's hand.

—There's nothing else to do, said Harp. This is how it is.

—Think of what we did, said Carr. We can't fix that.

The Judge and his second were eyeing Harp warily. Harp seemed to waver for a second. He half lowered the pistol. Suddenly, the second dived at the car. He snatched one of the revolvers from the hood.

Harp turned his arm. He pointed his arm at the Judge's second, and shot him in the back. The man sprawled out on the ground.

Harp turned the gun back to the Judge. The shooting had given him some strength. He spoke now with determination. The thing had started.

—You killed Lubeck, and you killed Brennan. Now it's up. It's up.

He pointed the pistol at the Judge's head.

—No!

Carr dove at Harp. He didn't think, he just did it. It wasn't fair what they'd done to the Judge and his wife. It wasn't honorable. They had a debt to make good. They had to give the Judge a chance to even things.

He struck Harp from the side. Harp fell beneath him, his pistol going off harmlessly. Harp was underneath him, breathing hard.

Carr struggled to his feet. Harp was cursing and getting up. Then a shot from behind him. Harp fell down again. The Judge was behind them. He put a bullet into Harp on the ground. Harp was writhing. The Judge put another bullet into him, and another.

—Stop it, shouted Carr.

He started for the Judge. But the Judge turned the pistol on him.

—Keep still.

Carr backed away.

—Stop it, he said.

The Judge knelt beside Harp.

Harp was crying.

Another bullet came then into Harp's head and there was just a mess on the ground where Harp had been.

—Can you see it otherwise? the Judge asked.

He straightened his coat.

Carr looked over at the Judge's second. The man was still alive, against the car, clutching at a hole in his chest.

The Judge put two fingers in his mouth and whistled. Out of the trees on the far side of the track came two cars. They pulled up. Out of one came a man with a black bag, a doctor. He knelt by the Judge's second and began to administer to him.

The Judge was quietly observing Carr.

—Why did you do that? he said.

—I don't know, said Carr. It was the wrong thing. I should have let him shoot you.

—But you didn't, said the Judge.

He moved as if to pat Carr on the shoulder. Carr pulled away.

—As you will, said the Judge.

He pointed to the cloth on the hood.

—Do you know what that cloth is for?

—No.

—It's for infants. Infants get wrapped in it when you take them home from the hospital. My wife bought it when she knew she was pregnant. Feel how soft it is.

He took the cloth and held it out to Carr. Reluctantly, Carr touched the cloth. It was very soft indeed.

The Judge threw it back onto the hood.

He took an envelope from his coat.

—This one, he said, is for you. Good day.

the seventh

Carr went straight home, and though it was early afternoon, shuttered the windows, lay down and was soon asleep.

A loud knocking at the door: THE WIFE OF THE JUDGE was standing in the hall.

Leon Carr?

She was wearing a thin wool dress with the same open tweed coat. Her cheeks were gaunt. Carr had never expected to see her. He had not arranged in his head any policy for how he would speak or act.

—I'm so sorry, said Carr. I'm sorry, I . . .

She took his hand in hers and looked patiently into his face.

Carr felt almost like crying, so kindly did she treat him.

—I'm sorry, he said again. Come in and sit down.

Then it occurred to him that perhaps she might not want to come in.

—Is that all right? he asked. Would you rather stay out there?

—No, no, she said. Here.

She came into Carr's room. She took off her coat and sat on the bed. She was staring at him and staring at him. Her dress was very thin, and he felt very much for her then. He felt he should not, but he did and he looked at her, there, seated on his bed.

—I don't know what to say.

He tried to think of something kind to say. He felt that because Lubeck and Brennan and Harp were dead the guilt had not gone away but was concentrated all on him.

But she drew him down to the bed beside her and took his hand. She slid it along her side and up onto her breast. She leaned in.

Her face was along his neck. She kissed him softly.

—It's all right, she murmured. It's all right.

His hand was along her and on her. In a moment, she had pulled her dress off over her head. She was pulling on his pants. She was on top of him. Her hair shrouded the room, and her lips were at the corner of his mouth.

They lay together there, in the bed, smoking.

—I suppose I should tell you, she said. There was no miscarriage.

She got out of the bed and put her dress back on. Carr was sitting with his eyes closed.

What did you say? asked Carr.

— There was no miscarriage. It was just a reason for my husband to fight you. He felt the honor of young men isn't what it used to be, and if there weren't some serious reason, you wouldn't bear up.

She put on her coat.

— I'm just telling you, she said, because you seem kind of nice, and I feel bad about the whole thing. If you like, you don't have to fight him. You can just go. Don't feel guilty, that's all I'm saying.

— This is . . . completely . . . why didn't you come sooner? Do you just let your husband . . . ? Aaaaaaaaaaaaaah!

Carr jumped up out of the bed and began to pace back and forth. She was by the door.

— Anyway, she said. Thanks for the good time. The whole situation made this rather intimate.

Carr looked at her helplessly.

— My friends are dead, he said.

— I'm sorry about that.

She opened the door and went out, leaving it open.

Now he was in the hall and she was gone.

They say that in a heavy storm one shouldn't be beneath trees for fear of lightning. Also they say don't go into an open field. This is very confusing, as, when I have on occasion been in a place of fields and trees during heavy rain and lightning, I become completely confused. At what point do I stay away from the trees? At what point from the fields? Do I dig a hole in the ground? Do I need to keep a little shovel with me for rain storms? In such a hole wouldn't the rain collect and drown me? That's not so much better and, in fact, would be much the same because I have heard that the bodies of people killed by lightning are bloated in a similar way to those found after a drowning.

Yes, Carr could not fix his mind particularly on anything. How senseless! What should Carr do? He felt very surely that he should go and shoot the Judge. Why had the Judge won the other duels? Because the others had felt guilty. They had let themselves die. Except for Harp, who was treacherous. Yes, he had been treacherous, because he had thought they had killed the Judge's child, and yet he had still gone on as if they were in the right. What if I were to go to the Judge's house and kill him in the night? Would that be the right thing? And now he had slept with the Judge's wife. Ordinarily a rather bad business, it seemed not to count for anything now.

The Judge's house was, as you might suppose, quite a fine affair. Already the cab was there. He hadn't even remembered getting in. And then he got out.

He felt immediately dwarfed by the house. This is one of the techniques of the very-wealthy. They make any-one who comes to visit them feel by virtue of architecture that he or she is a supplicant. I am not a supplicant, thought Carr. I am the aggrieved. I accuse.

He went up the steps. A man was standing at the top wearing a very comprehensive servant costume. Perhaps the man was a servant.

—I'm here to see the Judge.

—He doesn't know it, said the man.

—All the same, said Carr. I'll have my way. I have to see him.

—What you must do, and what will happen: they're not the same thing, said the man. It's my job to see the Judge isn't disturbed. All kinds of people come here after the Judge decides criminal cases. They feel they have been dealt with unfairly.

He pursed his lips, then continued.

—Unfairly, fairly. Who's to say that? Why, the Judge. That's why he's a Judge. So, whatever it is that you're here about, why don't you just run along.

He returned to his initial pose.

—Listen, said Carr. I want to see the Judge. I'm going in through the door one way or another.

—Well, said the man. If you are going to go, I won't stop you. But, I assure you, there are others more determined than I who are waiting inside.

Carr walked past the man and through the front doors of the house.

Inside, was a long entrance hall. A coatroom was on one side, with a man standing behind a counter. Before the doors that opened into the house, another man waited. Both wore the same servant-costume as the first man.

—Coat, said the first man.

Carr gave the man his coat. He felt like not doing it, but he did it anyway. In giving in to even one of these people's demands, he felt he was giving up some initiative. Nonetheless, he gave up his coat.

—Hold on a second, said Carr.

The man brought the coat back and held it out to him.

Carr reached into one of the pockets and took something out.

The man smiled encouragingly at him in a rather nasty

way. Carr sneered in return, but then thought better of it. He didn't want his coat mistreated.

— I'll be back for that.

— If you're not, said the man, we'll throw it away.

He held the coat mincingly in his fingers as though he preferred not to touch it.

Carr turned and walked to the next door.

— Not so fast, said the doorman, smirking meanwhile at the coatroom attendant.

— Not so fast, he said again.

Both broke into laughter.

— I need to see the Judge, said Carr.

— Don't let me stop you, said the doorman.

Carr went to go through the door. He tried to turn the handle. The door was locked.

— The door is locked, he said.

Both men broke into fits of giggling.

— Do you have a key? he asked the doorman.

— Do I have a key? the doorman asked the coatroom attendant.

—Yes, of course, he has a key. He's the doorman.

Both continued their giggling.

—Listen, said Carr. I need to get through that door.

He grabbed the doorman roughly and started to shake him. The man was very weak and small, and was hauled nearly off his feet.

—All right, all right, said the man. Here's the key.

He gave the key to Carr.

Carr put the key into the lock and turned it. The doorman, loosed from Carr's grip, ran down the hall.

—You'll get it for this, he said.

Carr remembered his coat. He started back for it.

No, he thought. They'll think I'm weak if all I'm worried about is my coat. And also, he thought, that man is a coatroom attendant. They must have some sort of code by which they never let anything bad happen to coats. Otherwise, on what might their pride be based? He decided to rely upon this coatroom attendant's code, and he went on through the door.

On the other side was a broad, curving, interior staircase. To the left a broad hall that passed by him and went off a ways to the right, just past a wide fireplace.

Where to go? thought Carr.

A girl in a maid's uniform was carrying folded sheets.

—Oh my, she said.

—Where is the Judge?

—I couldn't say, she said. But no one can go around unaccompanied in this house.

She dropped the sheets and ran to the wall. There was a bell-pull there. Carr caught her just in time, pulling her back. He had caught the back of her dress and it tore open. She lunged again for the bell-pull and it tore the rest of the way. He was forced to grab her about the waist.

Laughter came then from the stairs.

Carr spun around, still holding the girl, who now clung to him just in her underwear and torn-off dress.

On the stairs stood the Judge's wife and also three servant-men.

—You have quite an appetite, said the Judge's wife.

Carr let the girl go. She clung to him now all the same.

—What are you doing? he said. Get off me.

—First you assault me, she said, and now that you've ruined my virtue you want to get rid of me. I won't have it.

She held on tight. The girl was a bit too much for Carr.

—Get off me, he said, and shook her off.

—That's no way to treat her, said one of the servants.

—What's the big idea? said another.

—I just came to speak to the Judge.

Everyone began to laugh.

—A fellow like you, speak to the Judge!

A more ridiculous statement they had never heard.

—What's the idea in coming here? said the Judge's wife.

To the servants, then:

—Throw him out.

She turned and went back up the stairs. The servants came down towards him.

Carr picked up a poker from the fireplace.

The servants eyed him warily.

—I'm going up. You can't stop me.

And then his arms were caught up from behind. Someone had snuck up on him. The servants came up and took the poker from his hand. One slugged him in the stomach. He keeled over. They struck him a few more times and he blacked out. Then, he was lifted hand and foot and taken back out the front where they threw him unceremoniously on the ground.

Yes, that's where he was, mouth all full of dirt.

The servants had gone back inside.

Carr ran up the steps and into the house. He ran past the coatroom attendant and into the house proper. He ran up the front stairs and searched through the rooms on the upper floor. There were many rooms of every size and description. People were in some, and they shrieked and made horrified noises as he burst in and out. He ran and ran down the hall, which went on for perhaps one or two miles. He was continually forced to stop, heaving and gasping for air, before running on again. Behind him, in the distance, he could make out pursuit.

I must look quite a horror, he thought, covered in dirt and running about.

At the end of the hall was another stair. Up that stair he went and found himself in the countryside. It was a broad glad day and there was singing of birds in the air. A party of young men were coming along the crest of a hill. He went to meet them.

—We've just come back from the war, they said.

—The war is over, they said.

—Come and sit with us.

There were proud young women with them, and all were wrapped up in chains of flowers and summer grasses.

Over and over they kept saying it, it gave them such joy on their mouths to say it, *the war is over, the war is over.*

Carr laid on his back and it was then he remembered about his coat. He had forgotten it. He was on his way to, on his way . . .

He was standing again outside the mansion. The door was locked.

A cab pulled up. A slot in the house's front door slid open. The coatroom attendant stuck his head through.

—That's your cab, he said. Best to leave now. Here's your coat.

He stuffed the coat through the narrow slot. Carr took it. It was not the same coat at all. This was a coat he had lost once when changing trains, at least ten years before. This coat was far too small for him.

—Thank you, said Carr.

—Don't thank me, said the coatroom attendant. I'm not your friend.

The slot slid shut.

Was he outside Lubeck's house? Lubeck's mother was there, shepherding her children about. He could see her through the window. Then she saw him.

He was inside, and looking at her.

—Oh, this won't do, she said. You're such a mess. Come children.

So all the children took Carr to a great, castiron bathtub and together they all bathed him and washed him, and when he got out a fresh set of Lubeck's clothing was sitting there waiting for him. He put the clothing on. It was a rather nice pinstripe suit. The children gamboled and danced around him.

—Now you are clean and we shall talk, said Lubeck's mother.

Lubeck's stepfather was also present.

—It's much better to gather yourself before important conversations, he said. It just won't do for you to go about like a filthy animal. We don't live in caves, you know. Not anymore.

Carr explained what had happened to him.

Both were horrified. Around them danced and sang the uncomprehending little children.

—The man must be shot! resolved Lubeck's stepfather. I will go and be your second tomorrow.

—Thank you, said Carr.

—But this business at the house, said Lubeck's mother. And this business with the Judge's wife. Why did you take her up to your room and have-to-do with her?

Carr shifted uncomfortably.

—I just felt so guilty, he said. I didn't know what to do.

—Is that what you do when you don't know what to do?

Lubeck's mother and stepfather exchanged a look.

—What about this servant girl, asked Lubeck's stepfather. What did she look like with her clothes off?

—Stop it, you, said Lubeck's mother. That's about enough of that.

They walked Carr to the door, patting him on the shoulder and back and commiserating with him. They all felt very keenly the loss of Lubeck and Brennan. To be fair, they were not so sad about Harp.

—Treacherous cur, said Lubeck's stepfather. We should never have let him in the house.

The funeral was to be the following Tuesday.

—I hope to see you there, said Lubeck's mother. Brennan's family is going to travel the whole way, which will take from now until then and they will stay here for a few days and then return. You are welcome to come and stay here if you like. It is better in such times as these to be around other people.

Tonight, Carr told them, he thought he would rather be alone.

—That's all very well, said Lubeck's stepfather. We are all alone in the face of uncomprehending death.

Lubeck's folks smiled encouragingly at Carr as he went away in the clothes of their murdered son.

Then the dream shuddered, and he woke.

He was lying in bed, in his room. He went to the window and opened it. It was dark out. He'd slept the whole afternoon. The dream was muddled in his head, and sat with unconscionable weight. What was true?

He thought and thought.

The Judge's wife, he thought. She didn't come here. Then it was on him again. There was no lie. There had been a miscarriage. He sank to the ground beside the window, and sat back, curled against the wall. They were guilty. They *had* done it.

There was a knock at the door.

Carr went towards the knocking. Lubeck's stepfather was standing in the corridor.

—Thought we'd check on you. Everything all right?

Carr shook his head.

—Tomorrow, eh?

Carr indicated that the man should come in.

—No, no, I'm not staying. Just stopped by for a moment.

A thought struck Carr:

—What is the Judge's house like? Have you ever seen it?

—It's a small place, near the mill. A stand of birch trees, and a red house left of the curve.

I know it, said Carr. So that's the house. It's a small house.

—Yes, said Lubeck's stepfather. A small house. Are you going there?

—Not me.

Carr related the events of the morning.

—So, tomorrow. The track?

—I am, said Carr. I don't see a way out.

—I'll go with you, said Lubeck's stepfather.

—You don't have to.

—I know I don't have to.

—All right.

—Tomorrow then, I'll come here.

—Tomorrow.

Carr shut the door. The dream had now gone from him completely. He could no longer remember having felt betrayed by the Judge and his wife. His anger at the Judge was vanished in every extremity. In every direction, he could see only what they had done, he, Brennan, Lubeck and Harp, and how it could not be fixed.

No one explains this to you, he thought. That there are so many things without solution.

He lay down again, and lay for some time, with a blankness in his eyes before sleep drew him on like an ill-shaped coat.

Another dream, and Carr found himself sitting on the lawn of a great, landed estate. He could not turn around. He did not know why. Behind him, someone was speaking. A man was speaking about the construction of a cemetery, of black granite, of the need for the services of a particular sort of stone mason, of the rationale for certain wind direction and distance from the sea. Carr drifted deeper into sleep, and was gone even from his own dream.

He lay in bed. He could smell the morning where it was around him. A dog was barking somewhere in the building. A wind was blowing, and the house creaked. Doors locked shut strained to be wall, but they might never be. In a moment he had risen and passed out of the room. He did not permit himself to look at it before he left.

Carr was early. He was outside. It was cold. It was early to have gone outside. There were trees that lined the street. Each had been allotted an area of stoned-in earth. More than a hundred years ago, it must have been, for now the trees' roots up and down the avenue stretched and crouched and broke at the surrounding stone. The trees rose to make a tunnel of the street in summer. In winter the fingers met in the air all along, winding about each other. He felt the permanence of the street, of the town, the permanence of the trees. The wind came up again and turned him, pushed him a half step. He looked away from the wind. The sky was brightening. The wind blew harder and harder. He turned up his collar and sheltered against the house.

When he looked back, the automobile was waiting. He got in.

Lubeck's stepfather squinted when he looked at him, put the car in gear and pulled out into the road.

Carr looked down at his clothing. He was wearing his

best, a three-piece suit, an overcoat. Why? He himself could not say.

The car wound here and there. Lubeck's stepfather was taking a different route. Somehow this was a vague hope. He had never thought of driving in a different way to the track. Might that change things?

But soon enough, the ways came together, and it was over the bridge, through the curling country, and then up ahead, they saw, distinctly, through the starkness, a car and two figures waiting.

Lubeck's stepfather pulled to the side of the road.

—I'm sorry, Leon, he said. I can't stay.

Carr nodded. He patted the man's shoulder and got out. He could see through the trees the Judge's profile. The second figure was a woman.

Up to them went Carr.

He nodded to the Judge. He looked then clearly on the Judge's wife. She did not look very much like she had in his dream. This woman had clearly been quite ill. What must it have been like? he wondered.

—I'm sorry.

The cloth was laid on the hood. The pistols were there.

The Judge had turned away. He was staring off into the trees.

Carr touched his shoulder.

—I want to say, said Carr. I want to say I'm sorry to you both. We didn't know what we were doing. It's strange how luck can be so large and small. One turn, and everything goes. I mean . . .

The Judge looked at him wordlessly. The Judge's wife's face was drawn and pale. Her hand twitched.

Carr continued.

—I don't know what this is for you, what your life was, what it would have been. But this, it was something that happened in a street. There are streets and things that happen in them, and no one knows how or why. I want, I mean . . .

He looked around him. The day was now come completely

and the track stretched away. The trees rose up. The drive curved into the road which ran on and on into the town that he knew, and beyond. Birds sailed effortlessly between cold branches.

—I mean, he said. I mean . . .

The Judge's wife moved. She put her hand on the Judge's arm.

—Allen, she said. It's time. Let's be done with it.

He turned towards her, and his back was to Carr. Her eyes came over the Judge's shoulder. They were dark and small. There was nothing in them, nothing at all.

—Love, said the Judge quietly, he stopped the other yesterday. Hasn't it been enough?

Carr could not hear her reply, but the Judge spoke again, and then she spoke. She spoke on and on, her voice rising. The Judge turned back then, and his face was grieving.

—Take one, he said. Take a gun. Let's be done with it.

Carr took the pistol closest to him. It felt strange in his hands, smooth and heavy.

The Judge took the other revolver and went out onto the track. Carr followed.

The lines were still there where they had been drawn. A sickness was in Carr's belly. He felt himself thin and weak. He was walking and he was not. He felt that he was watching himself walk to where he would begin.

The Judge was where he would be. Carr heard the Judge's wife call out the signal.

Then they were walking towards each other. Carr held the pistol out in front of him. He pointed it like a stick and pulled at it with his fingers. He pulled with all his fingers and it went off. It went off again. The Judge was still there. They were at the lines. The Judge fired. He fired again. Carr felt his chest was hurting. He felt his legs hurt. He was firing, and the air was very clear. There was a hole in his chest. He could see it there. When had it happened? This was another thing that could not be fixed. Panic and his face white, and he was on the ground with his hands.

He could not see the Judge. He could not see the Judge's wife. The cinders of the track were in his hair. He could feel the track beneath him, and stretching out in every direction above there was a depth to the clouds that seemed very far and good. But then he saw that it was shallow. He felt very much that the sky was shallow, not a trick but something worse, absent all human ambitions. He thought that there were clouds and then clouds behind clouds, and then just air. Where is there that's far enough?

Then shapes took their places. Men were looking down at him. The Judge, the doctor. There was blood on the

Judge's coat. The doctor was saying something. He was moving his hands in a gesture. What did it mean? Carr felt if only he knew what the gesture meant, then there would have been something, some one thing to salvage from all of this. But the figures were become very small. One couldn't see them at all, no matter how hard one looked.

the skin feat

2008

1

I will tell you a thing, a thing you know, a thing perhaps
    you know
I will tell you the skin feat.
That I, of things relating, relate then this:
I was born—and die.
I am in between.
I leap in my skin and sew it to myself
and see how far I can follow
where leading leads
down under closed eyelids.

2

Every dream is startling to the dreamer. Yet when we
    wake,
we go about unsmiling—things don't surprise us.
Even when they do, we imagine we prepare.
But the world is sudden—that is its nature.

We must divert ourselves into a fence, into a button, into
    the ivy,
the grass, the fur of a coat
from which point we can judge and say—

each day I go ashore, and from what ship?

The skin feat . . .

Did I acquaint myself with it from a book?
Did I find it leaping headlong into water?

The skin feat is like the feeling of another age
in an ancestor, a grandfather's photograph. But you are
    not he . . .
you did not even speak to him.

How heavy arrival falls upon the house of the body.
It must contain every new thing that joins it—must
    consent.

We think that things are what we see—but our noses,
our ears, we question. Frantic being that glows without
    any light—
do you not feel it radiating from your face? You are los-
    ing it;
it is going away.

Those that love you agree—you will soon be bones in a
    wooden box

and someone else passing by, beyond the gate,
will glance at where you never walked, but lie.

4

The skin feat is an ascension of a ladder one carries in
    secret.
I speak to a man on the street, a stranger, I speak to him
    and think:
this is a messenger, a sort of letter that I may open in
    private,

and so I follow him, and tell no one. I do not document it.
It is not an art; it is for no one's amusement.
He goes down two streets, three streets, an alley,
a street, to a house. I am far away when he closes the door
but I go with him there, and vanish
and resound in myself returning
out of thoughts like barrel hoops—
like disasters one hears of on the road, and winces,
and in wincing, smiles at one's plight.

5

Is there a name I go by
if I wish to travel far?
My friend, this skin, like the crow's
feels the outer air even through locks.

And so we rush, my darling,
again upon the gates and are released, released

when wonder bids us die
and we refuse, and cease.

336

Yes, there are gardens that have been planted, and laid
   well
with stones for walks, and trellises, and arbors
and someone tends them.

I tell you this because I have seen them from a distance
and like the clockmaker, I do not understand
what grows without help in a place of safe keeping.

A house can have only one room. That is its character.

Larger than that, they are all palaces.

I feel I am, you know, like the building in a plague city
that up against a city wall, has, deep within
a door to leave the city.

The white scent of the sun cannot wake us, or else we
   were angels and therefore,
like pain, simply a message.

Our sleep is deeper—we cannot understand when it's
   explained—wildness.
we must fear it to feel it. One cannot oneself be wild.

9

Where wheels ring the lake a yellow word is seen at the
    corner of a child's mouth.
It is believed that things perceived as indistinct
are clear when seen up close —

but it is not distance that keeps them from us. A hurt
    mouth
reckons in equations of a thousand variables.

A hurt mouth is like a thicket, and cannot even be photo-
    graphed without error.

10

I learn to wear a coat in a particular way. I feel very
    carefully
the matter of my shoes —
I am setting out this morning for a funeral, my own
at a place not of my choosing,
a funeral as enduring, as patient as the cold beyond a
    door.

11

The worth of a saint is felt
like the weight of a tree of birds.
Wind learns its calling at the corners of the earth.
Longing so to return there, it never can.

And we—who when called upon,
cannot even leave the room we're in—

the one we've loved is calling from the hall
but we're helpless—rooted.
Where does a saint begin this freedom
of rising from a chair
to fall dead years later in a strange place
not a moment having passed?

12

Cavalry charges ring the house and grounds.
We learn to play with them, you and I,
in our speaking, our singing of the skin feat,
we learn to call
and have them come.

When you become better at it than I
then I am gone back into my book,
and someone is knocking at the door
of the room you're standing in.

13

Have you heard of a town baked into a loaf of bread
and given as a gift to one ungrateful?

Yes, streets, houses, squares—young men, women, dogs,
    soldiers.

I was told of it too late, and when I tried to retrieve it
I found it had been broken into a flock of birds.

Our dire attentions waver so — I wish for seriousness
and confront it in my sleep. But in the day it can't hold me.
I am desperate but of a sudden the windows are thrown
    open
and joy admits itself, like daring, all at once
pressing against me with uncertain gifts.

All these promises —
come with me to the field
come at this hour
and then

I want to believe and I do, but all my strength rises from
    the ground
and when I am best — when I rise in the wind, I am so
    helpless that I call to my love

like leaves in fear of rain.

14

The skin feat, beyond defying —

It begins as a loosening, a rise of the shoulders
the muscles prepare themselves but cannot be ready,
for the nerves go beyond them — out into the air
and the skin feat resolves as the eyes shut and open

and breath reaches to the horizon, the mouth
drawing in
something of ALL the air in the world
and feeling it there, in those small bottles of the lungs.

15

Red thread, blue thread, black thread, white thread.

I am involved in the thought of sewing, but I do not often
    sew.

Needles never glance—they are already through, already
    past
what is about to happen. But we,
obtaining for ourselves some lasting thing—we
are present where pretending has no joy.
What's childish is done without thought of the future.

Children's hands—can we call them needles?
Come with me, then, and turn your hands in a lathe,
lay them desperately against a whirring stone.

Out beyond the window there are crowds waiting
and waiting in narrow avenues of stone.

Cleverness is no salve. It wants too much.
It expects that it has won, or will.

You may learn to play an instrument, and carry it with
    you

and have it be a muscle, and always present.
That's what's best about people —
loving the world enough to confuse it for oneself.

But what is a statue? Can a farm be a statue?
Can a city? How long does a thing pause before it's static?

A camera with an open shutter in a high ceilinged room.
We pass by a hundred times invisibly.
I am invisible, you may say, in that photograph,
just as you say,
my wife is standing over there, behind that wall.

There is a door, and a screen, and then she.

Can you imagine what she's thinking?

16

The speed of trees must fascinate.
An oak tree on a slope releases acorns
and suddenly surrounds itself with oak trees. Oak trees
    are running
down to the water, they are running all along with the
    drive.
They ring a place. They drive from that spot in rings.
An old oak was there. It fell one day, in the midst of its
    dreaming.

You who write on trees, who carve into them,
be careful —

we must take care—
for, hold up your hand before your face—you cannot
    even see it,
so dark it has suddenly become.

17

A woman is torn in two by the skin feat. She takes her life.
She was on the edge of it. She felt it there,
but it was rotting. It had a stench.
I wanted to cry to her of the sea,
of wood that is called ash, of gas jets on a stove.

But pregnancy has no shape—that is its secret.
It isn't round at all—it goes beyond itself.
The sun is wrapped in a blanket—yet you feel it from a
    hundred feet.

Suicide is a carrying also—a pregnancy also.
One carries a cold word, a thought without shape
until it is possible.

One works as an expression of the limbs. Food is gotten,
so too a roof.

But there is no use to dancing
if you are yourself—
isn't movement a mask? isn't it a costume?
Are you so poor that you walk in only one way,
that you speak and act from one role?

Learn whole lexicons to people your theatre,
and surely know your audience
is no audience at all — just clatter
from a remembered hallway.

18

A bridge is being built. You may find the approach
a short walk from the place you're standing in.

There are you know, places where when you go there
no one can be admitted.

There are gardens like this — whole sections
of city parks, low places in forests.

What is it holds in a place like that, what matches
us so well that we, appearing there,
feel gone beyond ourselves, and knowing,
the sight of an empty landscape isn't human?

For we aren't human — not when we're alone.

19

The skin feat reports like a drum. Did I say it was
     breath?
It isn't breath at all — it's blood, the beating of blood.

We hear a drumming in the hills. We are out walking
and the drumming comes to us, and I do not look at
   you.

I am far too afraid.

20

But grief—are we not giving grief its place?

The skin feat is a wardrobe of costumes, and grief is the
   softest one,
as soft as a cooking knife.

We must love the dead, and learn to sense their finger-
   tips that trail
and never leave us.

And so, turning from them, we do not leave them. Grief
   is,
like age, a visible grain that runs the world's length,
but cannot be followed.

Violet glass of late afternoon when evening will be riotous.

21

Masts fare so well on ships—and how proud we are of
   them.
Nothing has ever been admired
as sails are, as masts.

The skin feat unfolds your folded limbs, your legs, hands,
    arms, chest.

Raise yourself in all weakness, not despite it, but in it.

We receive because of circumstance—not gifts, that's why
boasting is foolish. That's why

passing strangers in the early morning
you are not afraid

to look at their eyes
yes, there, where the light pours out.

22

But can you be covetous
of some costume you have made?

The skin feat does not set itself against things.

We don't frown on possession.

Who doesn't love, like a rat,
to fill the house with objects, to reflect our selves
in everything we feel kindred to
and gather that to us?

Only—let there be cycles.
Go one day from your fastness
out with a small sack. Five things you like
and you won't come back.

23

Am I afraid to be the way I speak?

One's hopes must always be larger than oneself. One
    must always
reach with thoughts where hands can't go.

The work of a life is to find something indomitable.

I love the color gray, and see,
how fine it would have been
to guess at fire, and to have been right.

The one who did that
had no thought for the future.

Be easy, be easy. Feel my paper hand
warm upon your own.

Do I love you? You are reading this book,
a book of my heart, and there are things clouding the air.

I expect that you will be hurt today. That you will be hurt
today, and the next day, the next and the next.

The ones who go through their hurt, they don't impress
    me.
Neither the ones who collapse beneath it.

Show me the ones who embrace it—who tie it tight
like a cravat, but unremarkable.

They cannot say afterwards even what prompted
that day, the necktie.

I am bound, they say, for a funeral, my own,
in a place not of my choosing

where cornflowers have been threaded
into a rope that anyone may carry.

25

We see animals and want what's theirs,
but are afraid to give up even one thing our own.

Don't you see? You're already carrying
as much as can be held. You have always done so.

Becoming does not mean hazarding what you were—
it means letting it fall away.

Each time you cross the room, you will step
delicately over

the skin of your old life.

I tie ribbons in my beard, on my wrists, my ankles.

Is it violence you fear? I have fought others and laid them
    down
and I have been hurt myself in the same way.

The body is so strong! It is covered in bark. It is poison-
    ous to touch!

I have also been a coward and stood by
and afterwards helped a friend pick up his teeth.

Do you see my tooth? he said.

I said, a bit of it is there. And there's another piece. He said,
the teeth break when they hit against the other teeth.

The sound of the skin feat is teeth breaking.

Do you feel the preciousness of your teeth?

27

Learning to be alone, well—that's the bell tower.

A child may have it—and then it goes away. You feel their
small hands.

They consume the very air.

But no one blames them. They are children, we say —

as if measuring the distance a body will fall.

28

Stones don't carry their own weight.
That's why they're heavy.

They are like impressions of another's sadness —
coming with nothing, you leave with nothing,
but we who despair are borne aloft.

Have you taken two knives and tried to cut one in half
    with the other?

I am like that when I'm hurt. I can't even
hold the knife-handles — I don't even recognize them.
I hold the blades and cut with sharpness into sharpness
and into my own hands.

29

We are so fond of our shadows.
There it is, we say when we see it.
There it is, my shadow.

Seeing your shadow is like having a conversation
when someone remembers something you once said.

It's like getting a letter, like waking on a boat.

We shouldn't really have shadows. Nothing
explains them, not really—

not why they're our own.

30

Will you sit with me, braiding?

I learn that tarpaulin is made from scars
and that oil cloth is carded sealskin.

I am always learning and I don't care very much what's
    true.

The skin feat—yes,—fares well without truth.

Unbuttoned like a coat, it fits as well with your best
    gallantry.

It is out in the sea with the long swimmers,
not when they're brave, but when they're weak,

when they're crying, with water in their mouths,
out of sight of land, despairing, wishing themselves
    seals.

But not the safety of a seal, no, the terror of it—
the wholeness of the world like a gray marble.

The sea is rising and yet we swim still deeper.

31

Our houses really are on stilts.

They really run on long legs of chickens.

We smell men hiding in buttons and would devour them—
or are you afraid to eat a human?

Are you so simple? There are crimes,
but that's not one. To eat a human?

Birds hunt all along the cliffs.
Our mythologies are numberless.
Did someone tell you all the tales were told?

I know another yet unsaid.
Shall I say it—already
another gathers in its place.

Myths are not a swelling of our lives—
they are not gold and lead.

They are sense—
the width of a board that you run along
from roof to roof
the street so far below.

Scarves pretend that they are nooses.
For them also the skin feat.

For them a white tinged joy of honeysuckle pressed to
    the mouth.

How long they wait, through a dozen summers,
through the growth of limbs, through boxes,
wardrobes, cupboards, shelves.

Finally, about the neck.
One can't imagine what that's like,
to be tied fast about a neck and gently there
to learn one's nature.

Were you once the hair on a sheep?
Can you remember so far?

You must behave as if you know what the others know.
But who are they? Did you even see them enter?

33

The skin feat is not a matter of consensus.
About this, no one will agree.

It is in spite of everyone. It is a weak arm that can't be
    bent.

Your mother sews you into a blanket.
Your father adjusts his hat.
The town gathers to see you off.

While awaiting the skin feat,
the audience convenes in rows and aisles.
But the theatre has been set fire!
It is burning to the ground.

Everyone races out. Six or seven are killed,
and one a child. But were they real?
Can you judge that? I am so slow in judging
who is real.

Perhaps they were just wriggling fish — or puppets.

Never again! the authorities say,
no longer can the skin feat be performed in this town.

They do not see that they are dancing wildly
in their best clothes.

And from atop a statue, a crow observes
and mutters; his beak is amidst feathers of no color.

For there are no colors inside a fire.

The elegance of older days is a matter of precedence.
Majesty has nothing to do with being clean!
I could sew a pretty countess into her dress
and myself into my skin

and we could run laughing, pulling
the one upon the other —

and what would it mean?

I should think a manual would be more forthcoming.
The skin feat is all intuition
like the moment of an arrow striking.
No one is shooting arrows —
they are just slamming violently out of the air,
driving into every surface — there's no shelter.

Barbed arrows — they can't be pulled out.

36

Life is just that —
emerging into dying. But you knew that —
were your parents not pioneers,
not the children of pioneers, no?

Build a house where there's no one to help you;
bury children;
or are you confused about the cost?

The skin feat comes only at great cost.
Its veins and nerves are bruises and broken bones
its melody the holes where teeth were.

Does it sound like a gray affair?
No—it is all wisps of light.

25,000 mornings, and every one leading promptly
into afternoon.

This is the skin feat—to hold yourself so gently
that you do not go to meet a friend you love
because you are remembering
the edge of something, and feel presently it will come.

Each time it happens, the world is wrought
where you are—
bells break in cold air.

Is it so small that you are disappointed?
I think you are not reading
through a noose.

No one is any better at saying what a feast is.
It's just the days you haven't eaten
hitting together like the bones of a necklace.

38

Are there really nations? Are there wars?

I had supposed we were all just pinned beneath rocks
on a long sandy coast
with birds to peck out our eyes.

We want so much to rise in the tumult
and feel ourselves grand and helping those who are
    hurt—
but we are between the walls of the house
where the world is made—
and can do nothing for the others.

Are you one of those who feels north is north?
Or do you suppose we orbit nothing in a void?
Is meaning itself a cancer—a lesion—a symptom?

Or can we learn to speak in symbols and disguising
our hopefulness
perish truly at the moment of death?

It is a chair that you have often passed
but never think to sit in,

this well-upholstered yellow chair
with thin legs.

It is crouching in its own space,
and counting quietly.

39

The saints who say that birds are angels—
they are so confused!

They themselves ate bread so long,
they have been good to others so long—
well,

we can plainly see the birds eat the bodies
of other birds.

40

Why, I am running so fast in this narrow lane
that I cannot stop.

I cannot even look back—not with my face.

And so, yet again you say, when asked,

I am setting out this morning for a funeral, my own
at a place not of my choosing.

With a telescope, you see from far away
what you will look like after a while,

but this
you cannot see:

for the plot is small, and it rains so soon after.

41

Yes, the skin feat! And my kissing of your hands!

I run out of the house to where you are standing with
   your bags.

I embrace you, I raise you up — I am strong
and you are very little.

You are coming to live with me. Everyone you know
has vanished in a plague.

UP and DOWN the halls of the house we go merrily.

I have made you a room, and set you a bed.
I have given you paper for letters — though there's no
    one to write to.

We will eat together and sit with wild thoughts mulling.
My hair is growing longer and so is yours —
my wife will shear it off, will hold us like sheep
and shear us.

I want to show you the town where I play my tricks —
for they are quiet tricks,

yes, quiet tricks
and no one knows I play them.

42

What ends this story of the skin feat? I find
I have explained it badly.

I worry that you will go back along this bridge of hands
and not carry my book with you.

The sun is climbing in the sky—
and out past the fence you can see figures
walking the road's edge.

I am looking now at the map of your life,
at all the rooms, the roads, the lawns and hallways.

You have dreamed of it, and you will dream of it again.

A light breeze blowing, a season ending—
you find a small house
and the windows lit.

Who is there, waiting, pacing the room?
Is it one, or many—are they saying your name again and
    again?

What is violent? What is beautiful?
What aches, what falls?

You are running and you will be caught.
Your very legs will fall apart, and you will still live.
And when you die others will forget you. So soon they
    will scour your name.

I tell you this because of my heart
that wakes me and wakes me

and wakes me with its beating.

Jesse Ball is the author of *The Curfew* (Vintage 2011), *Samedi the Deafness* (Vintage 2007), *The Way Through Doors* (Vintage 2009), *Vera & Linus* (Nyhil 2006), *Og svo kom nóttin* (Nyhil 2006), and *March Book* (Grove 2004). His novella, *The Early Deaths of Lubeck, Brennan, Harp & Carr,* won the Plimpton Prize in 2008. His work has been translated into many languages and work of his was included in Best American Poetry 2006. He is currently an assistant professor at the Art Institute of Chicago.

Milkweed Editions, a nonprofit publisher, gratefully acknowledges sustaining support from Amazon.com; Emilie and Henry Buchwald; the Bush Foundation; the Patrick and Aimee Butler Foundation; Timothy and Tara Clark; the Dougherty Family Foundation; Friesens; the General Mills Foundation; John and Joanne Gordon; Ellen Grace; William and Jeanne Grandy; the Jerome Foundation; the Lerner Foundation; Sanders and Tasha Marvin; the McKnight Foundation; Mid-Continent Engineering; the Minnesota State Arts Board, through an appropriation by the Minnesota State Legislature and a grant from the National Endowment for the Arts; Kelly Morrison and John Willoughby; the National Endowment for the Arts; the Navarre Corporation; Ann and Doug Ness; Jörg and Angie Pierach; the Carl and Eloise Pohlad Family Foundation; the RBC Foundation USA; the Target Foundation; the Travelers Foundation; Moira and John Turner; and Edward and Jenny Wahl.

Typeset in Cochin
by BookMobile Design and Publishing Services
Printed on acid-free 100% post consumer waste paper
by Friesens Corporation